THE BABEL RESURGENCE

BOOK ONE:

EMERGENT VISION

JEFFERY DALE COLE

To my loving wife, Melissa.
My partner in the adventures of life.
My muse.
My emergent vision.

PROLOGUE

Never before had the intentions of man reached so far into heaven. The grand obelisk on top of the tower seemed to be thrust straight into the heart of God Himself. It gleamed so, in the sunlight, that one might think it had light within itself, but soon sunset would reveal that arrogance to be the illusion it was. As it was, the celebration continued. The tower was complete and the dedication ceremony commenced. The platform atop was teeming with humanity. It took them a good part of the day to reach the peak of the manmade mountain, but even in the desert heat it seemed effortless this time.

Every time these people had ascended the endless stairs and ramps of the tower in the past, they felt the crack of a whip and strained against the ropes that defiantly pulled the great stones away from the surface of the earth into heaven. The journey finally seemed to be without weight or hindrance, apart from the pressing of body upon body as each one longed to be in the center. The crowd slithered around the great obelisk in the center of the platform for hours, like an ancient serpent never finding a resting place. The stench would have been unbearable if it were not for the trancelike state that fell upon them as they chanted and circled the massive obelisk, awaiting his appearance.

"Let us make a name for ourselves . . ." he shouted from high above the crowd as he stepped out onto the balcony jutting from the pinnacle of the obelisk. The crowd erupted in a roar that could be heard throughout the earth, or at least could be heard by most of the earth's inhabitants. This one man, speaking to them now, had hunted them all down and gathered them to this great city. It was this thought that occupied his mind and gave him the patience to wait for the roar to die down. He had something to say and, under normal circumstances, interruption was a dangerous or even deadly offence. To be interrupted by such praise and adoration, however, was certainly something he could excuse; for, although he would never admit it . . . even to himself, praise and adoration gathered to himself was his life's work.

No one really knew where he came from or how old he was, but his nearly eight-foot stature and imposing physique were seen as godlike in the ancient world. Although the fear for life and limb one felt in his presence played a large role in his rise to power, it was more than that; he had an air about him that was magnetic. He was deceptively charming and always able to convince those around him that his ideas were really the best thing for them, and that following him would be personally rewarding and fulfilling. It was only when someone saw through his rhetoric that he stood over the unfortunate soul and made threats without words. At that point, if one were to look into his eye, a darkness could be detected unlike anything in the natural world, and pure fear would bring the will into submission.

It had been decades since the massive foundation had been laid for the first step in the base of the tower. It was so large in its footprint that even the finished tower seemed to lie about its true height. The scale was so deceiving that one could be too far away to detect the other structures around it and yet feel as if an outstretched arm could lean on it, as if it were a wall only a few feet away. It was this kind of awe-striking deceptiveness that made the years seem to pass so quickly, strangely enough, even for those who bore the burden of the unimaginable labor.

Time always seems to reveal a nagging drive within the human spirit, a gnawing longing to be a part of something greater than oneself. The pain and consequences of self-directed, attempted fulfillment of such longing are often overlooked until the moment of catastrophic confusion—the moment when one realizes that the hole can't be filled by any natural means or human endeavor. A man-made mountain is still, in the end, nothing but a pile of bricks.

For those who could remember life before the tower, it seemed like yesterday that they were drinking in the elixir of promises flowing from the lips of this man of renown, this founder of cities and pursuer of men. Plans of a grand future flowed alongside rivers of blood and sweat. A future in which the mantra, "let us make a name for ourselves . . ." took on a life of its own. The cause had such an impact on the culture that if one were born after the start of the tower, their age was measured by it. They would say, "He was born in the year of the second step" or, "She is eight steps old." No one ever stopped to ask the question, "Who will be left to revere the name that we are making for ourselves?" Who indeed? The only one left to impress was God Himself. This man had gathered every soul on earth and put a rope to their shoulders for his purposes, and all the while, they thought they were making a name for themselves.

After what may very well have been hours, he raised his arms over the crowd giving the word to his royal guard to establish order by whatever means necessary. They had quietly positioned themselves throughout the mob and after examples were made of several people who were not heeding the command for silence, an unnatural calm fell. Everyone looked to the obelisk with what seemed to be one unified, glassy daze. He lowered his arms, satisfied that he had their undivided attention, along with their adoration and praise, then he started back into his speech.

"Let us make a name for ourselves! That has been the bed-rock statement, the cornerstone of this great society . . . The tie that binds us together and makes us one people, unified in speech and action, with one purpose! Let us make a name for ourselves! This one statement has gathered us here in this great city and kept us from being spread throughout the earth. It has kept us strong and safe . . . no more are we at the mercy of the wild beasts or in fear of the elements or of famine. No longer do we wander aimlessly after the wild herds or search for the sparse succulence of the wild fruit of the earth, nor do we glean far and wide the wild heads of grain, but with one voice and with right arms raised we say . . ." He paused as if he were reaching deep down into a place in the soul that not everyone has, then he let out a primal scream, "Let us make a name for ourselves!"

The power and emotion of his speech was too much for them at this point. As he screamed out the latest repetition of the mantra, the primal urge overtook them as well. The crowd erupted as if the mountain of bricks was a great volcano spewing living lava. It started as a chaotic rumble, and then it seemed to oscillate in and out of coherency. Suddenly, as if directed by an unseen conductor, it magically came into phase and revealed with clarity the words being shouted with one voice, over and over again, "Let us make a name for ourselves . . . Let us make a name for ourselves . . ."

Again, he allowed this to continue until he artfully sensed the perfect moment. There was no one on earth as skilled as him at working the crowd. At this point he could get them to do whatever he desired. For decades, he had convinced these people to put aside comfort and even life. Many had died of sheer exhaustion in the mud pits or on the long journey to the top with a burden of bricks. Many more had been trampled after slipping while straining at the ropes or had been crushed under a pile of debris from a poorly supported section of the construction. The power of such devotion . . . at his very fingertips, how would he wield it now?

With the tower completed, these people needed a new sense of purpose, a new impossible task. Perhaps he would demand a manmade sea in the heart of the desert? Perhaps a jungle spoken into existence and miraculously suspended above the city? With so many, so willing to do his bidding, maybe he would take a few and sacrifice them on the alter of scientific discovery. The birds would no longer command the skies. The fish would no longer mock from beneath a glassy barrier. No matter how many had to plummet to their death or plunge into oblivion, man would conquer the skies and part the seas. Even the moon would surrender to him. He fully intended to, someday, mount its pale gallop across the vast darkness. The possibilities were infinite as long as he could command the whole of humanity. With every idea, talent, drive, and ability at his very fingertips, the mountain they willed into existence would not become a monument to the past but a jumping-off point for a glorious future.

These very focused and determined thoughts of human domination were soon to be replaced by chaos and confusion as the ability to manipulate all of humanity with one silk-tongued oration would slip through his fingers in an instant. When it happened, it was as if he were a starving man who had finally caught a fish and then watched it splash back into the sea because he gripped it too tightly. What had taken decades to accomplish was to be blotted out of history in an instant.

The crowd below him was swaying back and forth as one while repeating the mantra, and for a moment it was as if the ancient serpent had finally found the elusive eternal resting place but was still content to dance to the rhythm of its charmer's flute. The sound of the recitation was like the singular voice of many waters converging into a powerful and overwhelming waterfall. "Let us make a name for ourselves . . .

Let us make a name for ourselves . . ." Over and over in one voice until, in an unmistakable instant, the clear voice of humanity fell back into nothing but white noise.

At first he thought the great chorus had slipped back out of phase, and he was annoyed that he had missed his cue. He was normally able to sense the moment just before their chanting would break into several competing groups. At that very moment, he would command a hush over the crowd, manipulating them into believing that disharmony was nonexistent in his kingdom. This time he was unable to see it coming. He motioned to the captain of the guard to come to his side, so he could give the special instructions that were required under these surprising circumstances. The captain complied with military speed and precision, finding himself face to torso with the gargantuan dictator. Although this position was always intimidating for the subject, it had its advantages too. It was almost impossible to look him in the eye while being towered over so, and to look him in the eye was a very foolish, dangerous game. The leader bent over from the shoulders, to ensure his command would be heard above the noise of the crowd, and ordered venomously, "Execute crowd control maneuver six!"

The captain started to sweat nervously, fighting the urge to look up at his face. Without understanding what was just said to him, the captain stared straight ahead in silence. The ruler raised his voice, to no avail, while returning to his full, imposing stature. He repeated himself furiously until the captain, in an attempt to comprehend, could resist no longer the urge to look into his face. Finally, he spoke up sheepishly, "Many apologies, Your Excellency . . . I can't understand you." This infuriated the despot. Not only that one would dare to look him in the eye, but that he would be further mocked by this gibberish.

Never had there been such rage in one individual. He thrust his arm out uncontrollably and grabbed the captain around the neck, as if he were being wielded by an unseen puppeteer bent on destruction. His hand was so large that he could easily fit two fingers and a thumb around the captain's neck. His other two fingers had to lay across the collarbone of his unfortunate victim and as he squeezed and lifted him up to eye level, the captain's hands instinctively grabbed the leader's wrist and then went limp as the collarbone of one side was forced down and the head was forced to meet the opposite shoulder. There was a gruesome popping sound as each bone was displaced and crushed. The captain was now nothing but a flag waving from the iron flagpole of the leader's arm. The leader dangled him over the railing of the balcony for all to see, thinking that this would bring about the compliance of the crowd, but it only fueled the chaos. He hurled the lifeless body down into the crowd, which killed many and started a domino effect like a living tsunami throughout the pavilion.

As people clawed at one another trying to get up, they shouted to loved ones for help, but no one could understand another. It was as if they were trying to hear the color of flowers, or taste the sound of a rainstorm. No matter how hard anyone tried, they couldn't make sense of any of the words in the air. As more and more people realized this, the noise and chaos grew to something much greater in intensity than what the leader had ever provoked with his rhetoric. Realizing this, the leader whipped around to face his advisors. They were all white with fear and could do nothing but turn and head for the staircase that seemed too small to provide enough hope for them all. The migration turned to a stampede as those closest to the giant were plucked into the air, two at a time, to experience his screams of rage face to face. His words were nothing but gibberish to them, and became their senseless, ironic eulogies. One after another was thrown into the crowd until, in ultimate desperation, the man threw his head back and his arms toward heaven and let out one final primal scream of defiance.

And the LORD said, Behold, the people is one, and
they have all one language; and this they begin to do:
and now nothing will be restrained from them, which they
have imagined to do.

Go to, let us go down, and there confound their language,
that they may not understand one another's speech.

So the LORD scattered them abroad from thence upon
the face of all the earth: and they left off to build the city.

Therefore is the name of it called Babel; because the
LORD did there confound the language of all the earth:
and from thence did the LORD scatter them abroad upon
the face of all the earth.

Ancient Text
(Genesis 11:6–9 KJV)

CHAPTER ONE

"Ten . . . nine . . . eight . . . seven . . . six . . ." The tower started to rumble and sway back and forth in response to the charming of the countdown. The rocket engines roared with the power of the will of humanity itself. As the countdown finished and ". . . liftoff" was exclaimed in a manner that seemed defiant yet joyful, the World News Network anchor broke in with commentary and elation that seemed strange for such an everyday occurrence as a rocket launch.

"It's a glorious day here in the desert as the sun gleams off of the pinnacle of the towering vessel that carries the hope and future of mankind into the cold darkness of space leaving behind a pillar of fire in its wake! What a beautiful sight! The rocket carrying the *Interpreter One* has lifted off and is on its way to rendezvous with *Epoch Utopia* where it will effectively complete the decades-long construction. For those of you just joining us on this historic day, let's go to Doctor Sorensen at the science desk for a recap of the project that has affectionately become known as *The Babel Resurgence*."

"Thanks, Bob," the doctor said as he forced himself to look away from the hypnotic sight and into the camera. "Anyone who has not had their head buried in the sand for the last twenty years is undoubtedly familiar with the construction of the great vessel *Epoch Utopia*, which orbits just above us. In fact, many of us have never known the night sky without it. What many may be unaware of, however, is the fact that its three huge outer sections and its central core were all four constructed separately by four different teams representing the four major economic unions. The vessel is meant to carry all of the diversity of earth's culture into space and therefore each section will be unique to the cultures that were tasked with its construction. What we have just witnessed here today is the launching of the device that, once in place, will interpret between the different languages and protocols used so that the ship itself will be able to act as one vessel and the different sections will be able to communicate freely. According to myth, humanity last came together, speaking one language and with the purpose of reaching into the heavens at a place called Babel, and so, we have *The Babel Resurgence*."

"A truly unifying event for humanity, Doctor?" the anchor chimed in rhetorically.

"No doubt about it, Bob . . . it even gets an old scientist like me choked up." Sorenson laughed only half-jokingly. "Some of our viewers may have been wondering why this endeavor has been nicknamed, *The Babel Resurgence*. I hope we were able to shed some light on that for them. We can only hope that this story ends better."

They both laughed, as if on cue.

"Thank you, Doctor," the news anchor chirped. "We'll be back with you in our next segment but first, let's go . . ."

Doctor Abus slid his finger across the video monitor screen from right to left turning down the volume. "Well, it's official . . ." He sighed to his assistant who was standing behind him at his desk as they were watching the launch. "I'm officially behind schedule!"

"I suppose that means that I am too?" she smirked and handed him an electronic note pad with the names and contact information that he was about to ask for.

"Apparently not, Lisa," he quipped back, always amazed at how she knew exactly what he needed and when he needed it.

"I couldn't find a current address on your first choice for Director of Colonial Development, but there is a link there for his last employer. It's two years old, but it's the best I could do. He seems to have disappeared from the face of the earth," she said apologetically and with a hint of sarcasm that seemed oddly out of place.

"He has a habit of doing so," Abus said fondly, trying not to lose himself in memory. "Lucky for me he's very gifted at reappearing as well. One time he led me out of a jungle so thick . . . never mind, I'm way too behind schedule to get into that story."

Lisa smiled and turned for the door. By the time Abus looked up, he only caught a glimpse of her short dark hair in the reflection of the still-swinging, glass door, bouncing away as if on a mission. She knew that if she stayed there any longer she was going to have to listen to another one of the doctor's humorous musings. Normally she wouldn't mind, but she knew he wasn't joking when he said he was behind schedule and it was her job to get him on schedule. As long as he had an ear he could not help but tell a story like that, so she simply denied him an ear while trying not to be obvious about her avoidance of this particular story. He thought it strange that she turned so abruptly and left the room, but he took the hint and scrolled through the list of potential candidates for the un-filled positions, wishing he still had the energy of youth that she radiated.

After twenty years of working his way to the top of ACTICORP and nearly another twenty of Palace service, Doctor Abus was put in charge of filling key positions on the mission crew by the Supreme Ruler himself. This was an honor to be sure but not one without its share of pitfalls. So far, he had avoided any negative attention from the Administration. With the myriad technical setbacks plaguing the *Interpreter One* team and the endless construction problems that the Physical Unification team had to deal with, his staffing problems were far down the list of things that would land one in the hot seat with the Palace. With today's successful launch, that was sure to change. The closer to completion the vessel and its computer systems were, the closer Doctor Abus would get to the top of the list. He was finding it harder than expected to find candidates that met the strict educational requirements while at the same time were free of attachments and agreeable to the socially engineered marriage and family arrangements.

It takes a special kind of person to leave everything they have ever known behind, even the very Earth itself, and fade off into the emptiness of space never to return again. Many of the world's finest minds were practically climbing over one another to be involved with the design and planning stage of not just the vessel itself but the social engineering that would have to take place in order to ensure a sustainable population in a confined space with limited resources indefinitely. They were all very eager to be involved in the planning but, as it always has been with central planners and social engineers, such people tend to exempt themselves from the implementation of their own plans. Strangely enough, this wasn't quite the case with the Supreme Ruler. Not that he wasn't demanding and catered to as any man of such power would be or not that he didn't hold himself to be head and shoulders above any man on earth, or in history for that matter, but this mission was his idea . . . his legacy, he himself will sail off into the darkness of space and into the annals of history and mythology. There are not many men so bold or delusional, as Dr. Abus was finding out.

The list of crew members that had backed out was longer than the list of positions that had yet to be filled and this had put the good doctor much further behind than even he had anticipated, knowing that he had taken on a nearly impossible task as it was. They weren't even to the test flight stage yet and candidates were dropping like flies—he tried not to think about why. He could only imagine what six months in space with a chance to disembark before the real mission began would do. The conscripts had good intentions, but people are at the very core social and sentimental. Leaving everyone and everything that one has ever known is nothing less than a supernatural task. He didn't blame them, in fact he had never come to grips with the idea himself. If he were of age to join the crew, he couldn't say that he would go through with it. After all, it was an insane idea put forth by an egomaniac in humanitarian's clothing. To launch oneself into the unknown reaches of space in an attempt to find the center of the universe? And to take a good portion of the population of the earth with you? The clothes of sanity are definitely missing from this emperor and there doesn't seem to be an innocent child in sight.

Dr. Abus had to consciously refrain from thinking about the insanity of it all. He picked his head back up out of his hands leaving what was left of his hair somewhat disheveled, removed his elbows from his desk, and scooped up the electronic pad that he had plopped down on the desk in frustration. Lisa's mention of his old friend gave him a place to start on the overwhelming list, an enjoyable place that hopefully would take his mind off the stress and madness of the whole endeavor.

He scrolled to the Director of Colonial Development position and found Noah's name at the top of the list. He pressed down on the screen over the contact link for his last known employer and the automated video operator for the university flashed up onto the screen.

"How may I direct your communication?" the 3D image posed in a manner meant to invoke nostalgia for a simpler, more personal age.

"Office of Administration, please," Dr. Abus said, realizing that the ploy had worked on him since he didn't normally find it necessary to be polite to computers.

"Live communication or information page?"

"Live, please," he said without realizing that he did it again.

"Video capable or audio only?"

"Video, thank you," he said, sarcastically this time, realizing why he wasn't normally polite to computers.

"One moment, please . . . You may leave a message with me if you would like."

"No, put me through now," Abus said, dispensing with the niceties.

"I'm sorry, sir, no one is available at the moment."

"Back-trace this communication," he said reluctantly. He hated throwing his weight around but at the same time, he couldn't help but enjoy the perks of being a Palace Appointee.

"I'll put you right through, Dr. Abus."

"Thank you," he said a little self-importantly.

"Dr. Abus . . . nice to see you. Sorry for the delay." An older gentleman came up on the screen. "I'm Dean Kent Stewart, we met once at an administrator's conference in Berlin. How can I help you?"

Dr. Abus pointed the note pad toward his office wall and flicked his fingers across the screen toward the wall. The 3D image was transferred to the wall and Dr. Abus looked up with feigned recognition. "Oh, yes . . . Dean Stewart. I'm trying to get a hold of Noah McAdams and I was hoping someone there might be able to help me?"

"Oh, Dr. McAdams. Yes, well he hasn't been with the university for, oh . . . about two years now," the dean said, trying to hide his disappointment that the Palace Appointee wasn't looking for him personally.

"Yes, I know," Abus said, somewhat apologetically. "But unfortunately, even with all of the intelligence at my disposal, I've only been able to track his last known whereabouts to your university."

"That's understandable," the dean said with a smile. "Noah is one of the last holdouts I know of who hasn't had an implant done. I could never get a hold of him when I needed to."

As the world became smaller and political power coalesced into one global system, there was an increasing need to overcome language barriers. The Supreme Ruler needed everyone to work together toward his ends, so he needed them to be able to communicate effectively. This seemed to go against the grain of historical despotic thought. To keep power, a central government had always tried to divide people into groups and keep them from communicating freely, for if the people were able to communicate freely and unite as one people, what would they unite against if not tyranny? He knew this all too well, so he gave freedom to them on his terms, in a way that would serve his purposes and be a means of control.

The most ironic thing about it is that he managed to control them in a way in which they practically begged for. He had a way of making people do what he wanted while making them think it was their idea and if there was any discussion or disagreement, one way or the other, he would convince all involved that it was really the best thing for them and that it would lead to their happiness. He killed them with kindness and convenience. He began a campaign which convinced people that the prices of privately run communication and information networks were exorbitant and that their decentralized nature was out of date. He also convinced the people that it was a matter of fairness that everyone, anywhere, no matter their personal means, should have the same ability to communicate and the same access to information. He went as far as to declare it a human right. His ultimate takeover of the world's communication and information networks began with the idea that these networks are utilities that exist for the public good and that it is exactly the purpose of government not simply to regulate but to run such entities. He de-privatized the communication companies and commissioned the development of a universal translation software program all to the great praise and adoration of the people. Access was offered freely to everyone, but he never allowed the code itself to leave the secure top secret government server. That meant that any user would have to have a live link to the server. It was that link that he provided for free—a tiny implanted communication device that not only allowed one to speak with anyone anywhere but in any language.

The convenience and the benefit to the people were obvious, but the real intentions were devious. He was able to create emergent behavior from groups or the population as a whole. Not only did he now have the power of thought and action of humanity itself, he could bend it to his will or wield it as a weapon. He had virtually all of humanity communicating freely while knowing who was saying what and where they were at any given moment, those who had an implant anyway. Those that chose not to get an implant were not much different. They still found it inconvenient to be without their external earpiece, and whenever it was with them, they were in the system too. It was genius to be sure but arrogant beyond precedent. He achieved the greatest control over the largest population ever by ignoring the most important rule of engineering: avoid, at all costs, a single point of failure. That kind of control can only come at great cost.

"Yeah, he can be frustrating sometimes, but I don't think an implant will cure that," Dr. Abus said about their mutual friend. "He barely says a word when you're having a face-to-face conversation much less over the network. Even when he's in the same room as you his mind is usually far away, probably in some jungle somewhere or maybe in some equation? It's hard to tell. Sometimes I'm not sure if actually getting a hold of him would make any difference." They both laughed unexpectedly.

"You know him, then?" the dean asked, surprised that Noah had never mentioned such an esteemed acquaintance. It shouldn't have surprised him so, because he knew that Noah was no respecter of persons. Noah had always treated everyone the same, regardless of social standing, unless one had no excuse for being ignorant. In that case he simply didn't treat at all. Noah could be best friends with the Supreme Ruler himself and never mention it to a soul.

"Noah and I go way back. I owe him my life many times over but ironically, I'm calling to ask him for his." Dr Abus's tone had changed from one of laughter to the more somber tone that one would have at an Irish wake. "Do you have any idea where I can find him?"

"I've only heard rumors really. Let me ask a few people and get back to you. I would hate to send you on a wild goose chase," Dean Stewart said, realizing the gravity of the request and hoping not to seem too eager to be delegated to by the Palace Appointee.

"That will do just fine. I'll put your link on the priority list, so you shouldn't have a problem getting in touch with me, and if I'm unavailable, my Chief of Staff, Lisa, will be taking my communications. I'll be waiting for your call. Thank you." With that, the viewer abruptly returned to default mode, not giving the dean the chance to enter into a polite coda of parliamentary farewell and appreciation.

"Thank . . . you . . . Doctor . . ." Dean Stewart was caught off guard by the abrupt end to their conversation, but he didn't let that ruin the slight power buzz he was on from having a direct line to a Palace Appointee. He was the direct opposite of Noah McAdams in this regard. He would probably drop Dr. Abus's name in "casual" conversation several times before the day was out and in a matter of weeks the students on campus would add ". . . when I was talking to Dr. Abus, you know, the Palace Appointee, that Dr. Abus . . ." to their list of humorous Dean Stewart mockings.

Stewart frantically brought up a class schedule on the now lifeless viewer, glanced at his watch, and dashed out the door nearly knocking over his secretary who was trying in vain to monopolize his attention for whatever time she could manage. "Not now, Maria!" he barked harmlessly, marching past her as if he was on a mission and forgetting to apologize for bumping into her. He flew down the steps, ignored the walkway, and cut across the lawn making the lawn-bot have to recalculate its mowing path. He arrived at the physics building a little out of breath but in time to catch Rajen as he was dismissing his Physics II class. Stewart wiped the sweat from his forehead as he impatiently waited for the students to clear out of the class doorway, then he burst in excitedly. "Professor Golkul . . ."

Rajen turned, a little startled from the energetic greeting, and put down his lecture board controller in order to extend his hand to the dean. "Dean Stewart . . . to what do I owe this honor? Did I park in your spot again?" he said jokingly.

"Don't worry," the dean said with a smile, "I had you towed." They both laughed awkwardly. "No, really . . . I just needed a few minutes of your time . . . on a matter of some importance actually." The atmosphere in the room seemed to become slightly heavier all of a sudden, like that change in humidity that happens just before it rains.

"Why don't we step into my office?" Rajen directed the dean across the hall, followed him in, and shut the door behind them. "Would you like a cup of tea?"

"No, thank you," the dean said, distracted by thoughts of how he was going to broach the subject.

"Oh, I'm sorry, coffee?" Rajen said apologetically. "Sometimes I forget what continent I'm on."

"Nothing for me, thanks." The dean paused as the two stared at the floor as if searching for instructions as to the next step in the conversation. "Rajen . . . you don't mind if I call you Rajen, do you?"

"No, of course, no," Rajen said, a little caught off guard by the dean's sudden familiarity. He motioned the dean to the chair across from his desk and they both sat down.

"You were good friends with Dr. McAdams, weren't you?" Stewart asked in a hushed tone.

"Still am . . . I hope," he answered only half-jokingly. He thought of Noah often since he last saw him two years ago. The whole tone and direction of this conversation was starting to worry him. He often wondered—half expected really—when he would get a communication with news of Noah's untimely demise. "Has something happened to him?"

"No, no, no, well . . . I don't know. I was hoping that you could tell me?" Stewart clarified. The tension in the room lifted a little but only for a moment. "When was the last time you heard from him?"

"It's been about two years," Rajen answered cautiously. The heaviness came back a little. For one thing, it was frowned upon by the powers that be, to say the least, for one to go off the grid, and on top of that Rajen had helped Noah gain access to a restricted nature preserve. He had a wife and children and couldn't afford to endanger his position at the university much less fall into trouble with the authorities. "Why do you ask?"

"Well, I was talking with Dr. Abus earlier . . ."

"Dr. Abus?" Rajen's ears perked up. "From the Babel Resurgence Project?"

"Yes, if you insist on calling it that."

"I wasn't aware that you knew him," Rajen said, trying not to sound overly surprised. If he had known, he would have made more of an effort to be on the dean's good side. Rajen had applied to work on the Project and even considered joining the crew, but he kept that close to the vest. It's a good thing too, if the dean knew that Rajen was circulating his résumé he would very likely make life hard for him. Not consciously, of course, Stewart wasn't a spiteful man, he was just overly sensitive. He took every little thing personally and it affected his attitudes and relationships. He tended to overcompensate for his insecurity by grasping on to any little thing that hinted toward approval or worth. He would then dwell on that instead of accepting that someone may not think highly of him. That often backfired though. One can only live a lie so long. Eventually, the façade comes crashing down and often wounds those unfortunate enough to be in its shadow.

The dean continued on, subconsciously allowing Rajen to believe that he knew Dr. Abus. "Yes well, we met some years back . . . anyway . . . it seems that he has some pressing business that involves Dr. McAdams and he is trying to get a hold of him."

"Pressing business?" Rajen queried, trying to seem merely curious while in reality he was starting to feel quite anxious about the whole conversation.

"He didn't go into any details, but apparently they're old friends and I guess he's seeking Noah's expertise. He probably wants him to help vet candidates . . ." The dean paused thoughtfully. "Did you know that they knew each other?"

"He never mentioned a thing to me and I'm his best friend, at least I was, you know, while he was here anyway." Rajen couldn't help but smile as he thought about it. "He sure is one strange bird."

"A bird that has flown the coop. Do you have any idea how to find him?" the dean asked.

Rajen tried not to pause too long before he answered, but his usually eloquent words were failing him for fear of getting Noah in trouble with the authorities. "Is Noah in some sort of trouble?" he asked cautiously.

"No, no, I don't think so . . . no. Dr. Abus genuinely seemed like an old friend trying to reconnect when we were talking earlier." The dean decided not to mention the offhand remark that the doctor had made about asking Noah's life of him. He thought to himself that that would only make things harder for Rajen. Subconsciously, Stewart was really worried that it would make it harder for himself to get any information out of Rajen. "Do you know where he is?" he asked a little more directly this time.

"Well, not specifically," Rajen said, finding it harder and harder to be casual about what he knew.

"Well, generally, then," Dean Stewart sneered, starting to show his impatience.

"He really doesn't want to be found . . . and, well, I'm his friend and I told him that I would respect his wishes." Rajen wanted to find him more than anyone. He missed his friend terribly, but that didn't change the fact that Noah did not wish to be found and he respected him too much to go against his wishes.

"I understand." The dean sighed. "But this isn't exactly an everyday circumstance. How many people do you know that are sought after by an important man like Dr. Abus?" he said convincingly.

"Well, at least one," Rajen said, lightening the mood again. They both laughed a little jealously. Rajen realized that Noah was being sought after and not pursued. Noah was the most brilliant mind that Rajen had ever had the privilege of knowing and it only made sense that the person in charge of recruiting the most brilliant minds on the planet would eventually come looking for him. "He's in the South Pacific somewhere," he mumbled reluctantly.

"Well, that is general then, isn't it?" Dean Stewart said sarcastically. "Is he on the surface or somewhere on the ocean floor?"

At this point Rajen's defenses crumbled completely and his shoulders hunched over as he spilled the rest of what he knew. "He's somewhere in the Ocean Preserve Archipelago . . . probably somewhere he's not supposed to be, knowing Noah. That's all I know, really."

"How did he get there?" the dean asked, not accepting that Rajen didn't have any more details.

"He caught a research vessel out of southern California whose chief scientist had a government permit to do research in the preserve." Rajen conveniently left out the fact that the aforementioned scientist was an old friend from college and that Rajen arranged passage for Noah in an off-the-grid fashion knowing that he planned to jump ship in the preserve.

"What was the name of the ship?" Stewart asked, trying to quell the excitement that came from knowing that he was about to get some information that would get him in good with Dr. Abus.

Rajen's face contorted as he tried to hold back the words that were about to spill out. He put his head in his hands and rested his elbows on his knees. "*Darwin's Pride,*" he blurted as if he were trying to hold back vomit.

"Thank you, Professor Golkul, you've been most helpful." The dean stood up abruptly to leave not realizing how rude that was, especially to someone of a different culture. North Americans tend to get right to the point and get on to the next agenda when they feel they have conquered the goal of a specific conversation. Dean Stewart was particularly inept in the art of conversational finesse which came naturally to people raised in many other cultures. To build up to the point of a conversation with niceties and often false interest in the state of one's family and affairs and then to artfully excuse oneself from the conversation with declarations of a desire to talk again soon that were also sometimes false, these were truly foreign concepts to Kent Stewart. No translation software could ever change that.

Rajen stood as the dean was leaving, feeling somewhat pillaged for information. He immediately wondered if he should call his old friend on the *Darwin's Pride* and warn him of the impending storm headed his way. He thought about it so intensely that his implant booted the contacts menu and whispered "searching" in his ear. "Cancel, cancel . . ." he managed to bring the command to the forefront of his thoughts. He decided against it for fear of his job, but his fears soon turned to the renewed hope of seeing Noah soon. That thought was almost worth the feelings of nausea that still lingered from his conversation with the dean.

Dean Stewart rushed down the hall, briefly looking back over his shoulder in a lame attempt to thank Professor Golkul one last time, but since he saw that he hadn't followed him to the door he abandoned the attempt and headed back to his office. As he was again cutting across the lawn, a couple of students waited until he passed and then acted as if they were scolding him for walking on the grass as no doubt he would have done to them if the situation were reversed. He was too lost in thought to notice them mocking him. He was struggling with whether he should continue to investigate Noah's whereabouts before he contacted Dr. Abus or should he call him immediately and update him on the situation. Calling him immediately would show that he was quick and competent but would risk cutting himself out of any further action on the Appointee's behalf. Dr. Abus may simply thank him for the information and take his link off security priority indefinitely. How could he update the doctor while still having reason to be in with him? Unfortunately, the dean didn't have time to solve this riddle because, like Rajen, he also had concentrated too hard on calling the good doctor and his implant was in the process of connecting him.

"Dean Stewart, I certainly did not expect to hear back from you this soon. Thank you for your diligence!" Dr. Abus was truly surprised and was not above rewarding diligence.

The dean was even more surprised because he hadn't completely decided to call or not. It took him what seemed to be an eternity to gather his thoughts and form words. "Dr. Abus . . . no, uh, thank you . . ." He wasn't completely sure at this point who had called whom. "I, uh have some . . . uh . . . in . . . uh information, uh that you may, uh that may . . ."

"Spit it out, my good man," Abus said, slightly more amused than annoyed. "It isn't bad news, is it?'

"No, no! What I'm trying to say is just that I have some information that may interest you." Stewart was glad that this didn't happen after he got back to the office in front of the monitor. He imagined that, between his quick pace, the heat of the day, and his red face of embarrassment, he looked as if he had just run a marathon. "I'm still looking into the details, but I wanted to be sure that you were up to speed." He lied, hoping to cover up his bumbling.

"What have you?"

"Well, I found out for sure that he joined the crew of a research vessel that sailed out of southern California." Stewart paused not wanting to give up too much information too soon.

"When was that?" Abus asked with increasing interest.

"Uh, about the same time he left the university."

"What was the name of the ship?" Abus pushed, sensing that the dean was holding back for some reason.

"Well, I still have some details to look into . . ."

"Look, Kent . . . may I call you Kent?" Abus said, hoping to disarm him a little with feigned familiarity.

"Yes, of course."

"Kent, I'm very appreciative of your help and I won't forget it. Just tell me what you know and I'll be sure to put a good word in for you with whomever you wish. Certainly a competent administrator like yourself has ambitions of some sort?" Abus laid it all out there hoping to save time and endless negotiating.

Stewart was caught somewhat off guard and didn't know where to begin. "Thank you, Dr. . . . I, uh . . . I don't know what to say . . ."

"How about starting with the name of the ship?" Abus continued to push.

"*Darwin's Pride*," the dean blurted before he even knew what he was saying.

"Where was it headed?"

"The science officer had a permit to do research in the Ocean Preserve Archipelago. I know that it's a vast region, but I'm sure with the name of the ship we should have no problem locating him." The dean artfully included himself in the rest of the quest.

"I'm tracking it as we speak," Dr. Abus replied, hinting that he would no longer be needing the dean's help. "Is there anything else you had for me, Kent?" he said, giving Stewart one last chance to cash in on his offer or let an important detail slip.

"Well, I'd be more than happy to track him down for you myself," Stewart offered sincerely.

"No, actually this is the one candidate that I am looking forward to finding myself. Thank you again, Kent."

"Are you sure that there is nothing else I can do for you?" Stewart almost begged.

"No, no, but if you find out any more details or, as I mentioned before, if you need a reference from my office or anything, I'll leave your security clearance high enough to reach my assistant Lisa." He tried to be as polite as one can be while telling someone else that they're not important enough to talk to any longer.

"Thank you, Doctor," Stewart managed to get in this time before he heard the end communication indicator. Dean Kent Stewart slowly lumbered back to his office, heavy with thoughts about how he could take advantage of this opportunity to redefine his life.

Doctor Barnard Abus felt reborn in his efforts and seemed to float out of his chair as he stood to walk toward the door to Lisa's office. Before he even spoke, she could tell he was on a roll and would be throwing out impossible requests with few details, so she made a mental note of where she was in her current task and turned her focus fully to him.

"Lisa, I need to get to the South Pacific immediately."

"Your transport is fueling as we speak," she said, almost interrupting him.

"How do you do that?" he marveled.

"Supernaturally!" she chirped with a smile. It helps that she is always listening to his conversations in the background as she works, but there was no need to tarnish her reputation as a miracle worker by bringing that up.

The fact that it did now take three people to do the job she originally did when she first came on board attested to the fact that she was comparatively, a miracle worker. It did not take long for Dr. Abus to recognize her talent. As she gained the confidence of the Cabinet Secretary, he continued to promote her and eventually gave her the official title of Chief of Staff, much to the chagrin of the older staff members who had been with him much longer. She was only in her early thirties, but she was addressed by most everyone in the Administration as Madame Chief of Staff or just Ma'am to those in the office who had to interact with her on a daily basis. Only her closest confidants, of whom there were few, called her Lisa and, of course, Dr. Abus and anyone he introduced her to as "his assistant, Lisa." He was oblivious to the potentially demeaning nature of that term, but it was the most accurate description of her role. She was to assist him in any and every way, a virtual extension of himself and his own authority.

As she hired people to do the things she no longer had the time to do herself, she very wisely kept tight control of two tasks personally: his calendar and his communications. To the rest of the world, those two things were, in essence, him.

It was actually almost supernatural that she sensed that he would want to go in person this time. These days he very rarely left the capital, but there was something in the way he had been reminiscing about his old friend that told her that if there was anyone he was going to go and recruit in person, it was Doctor Noah McAdams.

CHAPTER TWO

The weight of thousands upon thousands of souls pressed in from all around him. The heat and the stench were hellish beyond imagination and there seemed to be no escape from the throng. Pushing, shoving, clawing, all trying to be in the center . . . get to the center . . . get to the center . . . at all costs find yourself in the center . . . no escape . . . no hope. Wait! What was that? A glimpse of hope . . . who was that? I know that face . . . in the crowd, there. Gone! There it is again, over there. No, don't go! Too late . . . gone again! Spin around . . . push, claw your way . . . there it is, no . . . there she is, yes, it's her face! As soon as he realized it was her face, he started floating above the mob as it slithered around and around, orbiting the gigantic obelisk. The noise of the crowd was thunderous as it swirled and billowed . . . billowed white . . . white smoke . . . it's smoke, not people! Are they burned? No, no . . . where are they? The obelisk? It's shaking, swaying, shimmering . . . the corners . . . crumbling, falling off, revealing the truth . . . it's not stone . . . it's round, glimmering . . . shining metal . . . rising, slowly at first . . . rising, faster and faster . . . it's rocketing toward him . . . he can't escape . . . if only he could see her face one more time he knew it would be okay. Where is she? Please! No! Come back! The noise was unbearable . . . fire, too bright to look at . . . shaking, thunderous cloud—

"No!" Noah screamed and sat straight up in his hammock nearly dumping himself onto the hard, bamboo floor. He instinctively put his hand up to shield his eyes from the falling sun that had tortured him in his sleep. He was still unsure if he was awake or asleep as the swirling cloud was still there. As he closed his eyes to keep out the blowing sand, he brought his hands quickly to his ears to protect them from the awful noise.

As vertical takeoff and landing aircraft go, historically, this one was relatively quiet, but at such close range it was loud enough to rouse a deaf, dead man from eternal slumber. The craft circled slowly just above the tree line as if it were stalking him. Suddenly, it darted up the beach about one hundred meters and, from out of nowhere, a second craft took its place. Even more sand and sea mist joined the tempest about the small structure as the second craft took its place over the water, just off the beach. It hovered for a moment, then, just as suddenly as the first, it screamed down the beach in the other direction, about one hundred meters.

Noah recognized this maneuver as the precursor to a military securing of the beachhead between the two aircraft, the focal point of which would be his little beach hut. He slipped out the back of the structure, under cover of the jungle canopy, as the hut was right in the shade of the tree line at the top of the beach. Instinctively, he crouched to the size of a boar and scurried straight back until he hit the game trail that paralleled the beach. He followed the trail down the beach toward the position of the second craft, hoping he could get out of the target cone before they had boots on the ground. He knew if they had spotted him in the hut, however unlikely that was, they would be expecting him to continue fleeing straight back, deeper into the jungle.

Whoever they were, they were displaying military tactics, and even the aircraft themselves, unmarked as they were, betrayed a well-funded and professional operation. Noah was sure they would be equipped with tracking equipment, but fortunately for him, the daylight would work in his favor. Their night vision capabilities would have no problem zeroing right in on him, no matter how dense the jungle, but the temperature and humidity on this little island were ideal camouflage for a large mammal trying to evade an infrared scan. He was hoping that if he continued to mimic the silhouette of a small animal he could slip past them and be free to think about his next move.

Time to think did not come as he had hoped. By the time he had reached the second craft, it had already landed and there was a line of camo-clad figures racing into the jungle. Noah shot up the nearest tree like a cat being chased by a pit bull, being careful to keep the tree between himself and his uninvited guests. From this vantage point, he could detect the distinct squad formations breaking out of the uniform penetration into the jungle. One squad continued to hold the line perpendicular to the beach while stretching it as far into the jungle as they could without losing line of sight with each other. The other started a push line toward the hut, also spreading as thin as they could, to cover more ground. As the push line closed in on Noah's position, the perimeter line pivoted so the end that had penetrated deepest into the jungle would ultimately meet up with their mirrors from the other craft, forming a triangle with the beach, from which there was no escape. They moved silently for how swift they were moving, but Noah knew every sight and sound of this forest the way a mother knows the different meanings of the crying of her child. He could detect the straight lines, the synchronized movement, and the other patterns not indigenous to this island that they where inflicting upon it in their hubris, but that was clearly not going to be advantage enough for him to escape the ever-tightening vise closing in on him.

The push line reached Noah's position and by this time they had spread themselves very thin. Noah's pupils were wide like a predator, and the adrenaline rush brought on by the proximity of the invaders caused a slight shiver up his spine. That shiver was always the last thing Noah felt before he did something reckless. He very rarely did anything stupid, but recklessness was one of the tools of his creative genius. While others would heed the warning of that little shiver up the spine and step back from a ledge or back down from a conflict, Noah would interpret it as the body gearing up for greatness. For Noah, it was like the excitement of a starting gun, not the fear of the end of a gun.

Noah noticed the two-dimensional thinking of the two grunts closest to him, seeing that they scanned the forest in front of them left to right but rarely, if ever looked up. That meant he could probably remain concealed in the tree above them as they passed by, but he would still be within their secured perimeter and Noah was not one content to sit and hide. What he really needed was some intel, and his insatiable need to know soon found opportunity to strike. The man closest to him used the very tree Noah was in for back cover, placing the tree between himself and the aircraft he came from, just as Noah had done. Noah could barely see the next grunt in the line from his elevated position, which meant that the men could not likely see each other at ground level, a temporary situation for sure. They were trained to reestablish contact on regular intervals. Noah waited for any sound or body language indicating that contact had been made while watching the sweep pattern of the next man.

As he waited, he reached into the deep pocket of his shorts and pulled out a small bamboo case. The carefully constructed case was to protect him from the sharp points of the homemade blow darts inside or more importantly from the neurotoxin he had coated them with. He carried the darts and a long blowgun with him whenever he roamed the island to always be ready to take down a boar if the opportunity presented itself, but in his haste, he left the blowgun leaning against the corner post of the hut on the beach as he fled the unknown invaders.

When the moment of contact between the two squad members came, Noah felt that shiver up the spine once again and pounced silently on his prey. The grunt didn't know what hit him. Noah rained down from above as silent as a cat and stuck the soldier in the neck with the dart as he landed behind him. The paralyzing toxin took effect immediately, as it was dosed to take down a hundred-and-fifty-kilogram boar. Noah supported the limp body before it had a chance to collapse to the ground while taking special care not to make any unusual sound or place himself in the soldier's line of sight since military implants transmitted visual as well as auditory data. As Noah had hoped, the man's eyes did not even close so everything he was seeing was still being broadcast by his implant to operation HQ, wherever that was, and they were, hopefully, none the wiser.

As Noah had feared, the military implant made external means of communication obsolete leaving him with no way of monitoring communications to gain the intel he was now in desperate need of. The only thing he could do now was continue to move the limp body toward its intended goal to buy more time to locate an escape route.

He managed to stay camouflaged enough at ground level to convince the next squad member over that it was indeed the soldier he was carrying that was returning his periodic contact signal. There was no one to the other side because the man he was carrying was tasked with keeping the beach in view, and the gunners on the aircraft had clear line of sight to one another down the beach with Noah's hut targeted halfway between them. Making a run for the water was tempting, but Noah was too smart to give in to something as panicky as that.

Before he knew it, he was back at the hut. The push line he was a part of happened to reach the hut first, but it would only be moments before their mirrors would meet up with them.

The squad leader must have indicated an all clear because out of nowhere screamed a third aircraft which started to circle as if to stake a claim on the beach in front of the hut.

Out of options, Noah propped his unwitting passenger up against the nearest tree and slipped back into the hut as if he had never left. He convinced himself that he was simply changing tactics from escape and evade to diplomacy and not admitting defeat.

Noah could only make out the silhouette of the latest aircraft to arrive through the blowing sand as it passed in front of the sun. He hurried to the edge of the raised floor and grasped the corner post of the open walled structure with one hand while shielding his eyes with the other. He desperately searched for markings on the vehicle in a further attempt to satisfy the questions flashing through his mind like lightning. After a few moments, in his typical manner, Noah filed all of the questions away in his mind, took a deep, cleansing breath and calmly focused on gathering information, a practice that had often saved his life. He stared intently at the craft until it finally slid out from in front of the sun and hovered over the beach just in front of his hut. He was able to make out the palace seal on the side of the aircraft as it spun and landed on the wet sand.

A whole new set of questions now flooded his mind like the adrenaline that was flooding his bloodstream. Noah couldn't imagine why such a vehicle would be landing on his beach. He was expecting to, someday, have to deal with the Parks Department or the World Environmental Protection Agency but not the Administration. He couldn't decide if he was in more trouble or less, and at this point curiosity seemed to trump fear. He found himself strolling toward the machine mindlessly as the cloud of dust settled around it.

He must have looked as if he had just walked through a vortex in time to those on the aircraft. His long, unkempt hair and full, out-of-control beard along with his sun-darkened, lean, muscular, half-naked body gave him a primitive, almost prehistoric look. If it were not for his handmade shorts, woven from hemp-like plant fibers he had discovered on the island, he could have been mistaken as simian. Even the dumbfounded expression on his face as it framed an innate look of intelligence in his eyes was deceptively ape-like.

The two worlds that he had managed to keep apart for so long were suddenly thrust together as the door of the aircraft slid aside and a khaki-clad figure in an old panama hat emerged. As he started out toward him, Noah could not shake the odd feeling of familiarity that had come over him. He realized that it was emanating from the silly hat atop the purposeful yet slightly comical gait. An uncharacteristic serge of emotion swept over Noah as the funny little figure raised his head so that the brim of the hat no longer obscured his face.

"Barney . . . is that you? You ol' son of a . . ." Noah could hardly contain his joy but yet still managed to tame his language, leaving others to be responsible for filling in whatever descriptive metaphors they felt comfortable with.

"So . . . you're not dead!" Dr. Abus shouted over the dying whine of the aircraft engines as the old friends embraced like athletes who had just won a championship. Noah was the only one on earth that got away with calling him Barney, and he had forgotten how much it amused him.

"Almost!" Noah laughed. "What are you doing here?" He gasped with all of the emotion of a man who had not seen another living soul in two years. It surprised even Noah how much the solitude had affected him. Noah had always been a solitary man, but even he was not unaffected by the lack of seeing another human face or hearing another human voice. It was beginning to affect his dreams. Lately they were so vivid that it was as if he were really seeing, hearing, and speaking with the people appearing there only for them to dissipate into phantoms of memory as he awoke to his still surreal life. He didn't mind so much when they were dreams of Ruth.

Although, it was his regret regarding his relationship with her that was the only thing that ever made him feel like a castaway trapped on this island with no hope of rescue, so even good dreams seemed to torture him. He temporarily brushed aside hopeful thoughts of seeing her again to focus on listening to Barnard's explanation of his grand entrance.

"Looking for you! What, did you think I was on holiday?" Barney slapped him on the back several times ignoring the odor of natural man as the embrace went on longer than either was comfortable with.

"How on earth did you find me?" Noah said, trying not to think too hard about the implications of that question.

"Well, it wasn't easy . . . let's just say it involved a little cajoling, some bribery, and technology that I can't discuss with you at your current level of clearance." Barney smiled knowing that Noah understood that he was being funny but was not in any sense joking.

They were distracted momentarily as Abus had to wave back the security detail that seemed to be waiting for any opportunity to shoot something or someone.

"Don't worry," Noah said reassuringly, "I'm the largest carnivore on this island . . . it's quite safe, well it is for everyone else except your one man you'll find propped up against a tree behind the hut. Sorry about that. He'll be okay after a few hours; he's just paralyzed temporarily. Believe me, there is no one else here. I know every inch of this place."

"Oh, don't mind them," Abus said, a little annoyed with his security detail while practically ignoring that Noah was somehow able to take one of them out. "They haven't tackled anyone since we left the capital. They get a little restless when we travel." He gave the agent in charge a cold glare; the agent then brought up the all-clear command on his military-grade eye implant and sent it to the rest of the squad. They diverted their attention from Dr. Abus's immediate proximity to the jungle tree line. Abus then continued with the conversation. "Let's talk."

"Well, you're just in time for tea. Come on in to the parlor." Noah motioned theatrically and led him up the beach. Barney started toward the hut where Noah had been napping, thinking the little shack was the extent of the hospitality Noah had to offer him.

"Not here." Noah smiled. "This is just the beach house. Let's go up to the mansion." His smile seemed to resemble the cat that ate the canary. "It's not far, besides we wouldn't want those jungle fatigues to go to waste, now would we?"

Barney was delighted by the prospect of once again following Dr. Noah McAdams through the jungle. As they reached the edge of the tree line, a small trail came out of hiding and as soon as he saw it, Barney realized Noah would never make a permanent camp below storm surge level, especially in the tropics. His thoughts were interrupted by a cheery "heads up" after Noah had grabbed a piece of fruit off a low-hanging branch and tossed it over his shoulder as they walked. Barney fumbled it a few times but finally managed to catch it and rub it against his shirt as if he was simply trying to shine it up all along. He didn't know exactly what it was, but he took a large bite and was overcome by the purity and freshness. He moaned involuntarily as juice dribbled down his chin while trying to remember the last time he had a piece of fresh, wild, non-engineered fruit. He made the mistake of trying to talk with his mouth full as Noah cut him short.

"Save your breath . . . you're going to need it for the last leg. We'll have plenty of time to talk once we kick back with a nice cold drink," Noah said with that same devious smile. Barney chuckled, thinking he was kidding. Noah unknowingly picked up his pace and even the security detail was having a hard time keeping up. He was torn between the anticipation of having an intelligent conversation with something smarter than a monkey and the desire to show Barney what he had created on this primitive island paradise. The last leg of the barely recognizable trail angled up the side of a steep ravine, and after several switchbacks Barney was grateful for the lack of conversation. He could hear the sound of rushing water getting closer and closer and it was making him think more seriously about that cold drink Noah had offered him. He was about to stop and hit his security chief up for a swig from his canteen when the slope suddenly flattened out in front of them to reveal a sight that took his breath away more than the climb itself.

The side of the cliff plateaued briefly and then shot skyward almost vertically next to a one-hundred-foot waterfall. As they walked closer he could see that after pooling briefly on a lower, eroded portion of the flat, the water continued to fall another fifty feet or so into the ravine below. He had never seen anything so beautiful and it had captured his senses so, that he was completely unaware of the magnificent architectural achievement they were standing next to.

"Come on in," Noah said as he started up the stairs.

Barney turned his head toward the sound of Noah's voice, but his eyes followed reluctantly as he was under the spell of the beauty of nature. As soon as his eyes caught up with his head, he gasped at the unbelievable sight of the beauty of man's creation.

The house was not large since it was built by and for only one man, but it was exquisite hand-made craftsmanship. The roof was a simple gable style, but the intricate system of troughs made from turned-up bamboo halves overlaid with the other halves turned over atop the seams with one on top running the entire ridge, was not only aesthetically pleasing but necessarily functional. The system didn't simply provide solace from the torrential tropical downpours of the region, but it also collected and stored the fresh water through a series of bamboo gutters and storage tanks turning the storm clouds into showers of blessing. Unlike the beach hut, this home had walls and beautiful, smooth floors. The floor of the beach hut was simply small diameter, young bamboo shoots overlaid on a simple girder system. It was rough and uneven and primitive. The floors here were flat, smooth, and polished. Noah had taken large diameter bamboo, cut it into sections small enough to steam and flatten with a pressure jig he had built. It was as fine as any hardwood floor made back in civilization and more beautiful and durable because of the finish he had made from tree sap and other plant extracts.

The walls were made in a way that allowed Noah to completely close the house up during a storm or almost completely open it up to the natural breeze created by the giant waterfall meters away. The location of the house against the cliff face next to the falling water was to make use of the natural air conditioning created by the moisture and the constant movement of the air. The wind tunnel effect also served to keep insects away, practically eliminating the need for screens or mosquito netting. The placement of the beach house was to make use of the same principle. Noah had built that on a small peninsula when he first arrived to make use of the constant sea breeze that raced around the island at that point. He still enjoyed napping there after fishing or an afternoon swim though he moved up to the main house some time ago.

Barney followed Noah up the steps almost tripping because he couldn't make his eyes decide where to focus. It was all so beautiful. The shining floors became a canvas for the art of the woodwork exploding up to the cathedral ceilings through the massive pillars. Above the main floor there was a balcony with an exquisite railing that seemed to defy the primitive capabilities Barney knew Noah had been limited with here.

"How about that cold drink now?" Noah offered with a sincerity that, again, defied the primitive conditions.

"Please . . ." Barney managed to whisper with less disbelief.

Noah walked to the far side of the floor into what could be described as the kitchen and pulled two glasses down out of a cupboard. He placed the glasses on a small counter and grabbed a coconut and some of the fruit Barney seemed to enjoy from a wooden bowl on the table behind him. With military precision, he swung a machete from out of nowhere, scalping the coconut just enough to create a pour opening and without spilling a drop. He poured an equal amount of the milk into each glass and skillfully juiced one fruit in each. He then added a mixture of noni and mangosteen juices left over from breakfast and theatrically prepared for the final touch to his creation.

"Now for the secret ingredient." Noah smiled as he pulled the stopper off the top of a blown glass flask and passed it under his nostrils. He splashed a little in each glass and then opened the top of a curious-looking box next to the counter. With another swing from the mysterious machete, there was a sound that resembled breaking glass. Noah plunged his hand into the box and it emerged gingerly grasping several pieces of clear, refreshing ice.

The sound of the ice hitting the glasses was like music to Barney's ears and his dumbfounderment now took a second seat to his thirst. Noah handed him a glass after swirling it around to mix the tropical liquid with the arctic miracle. Barney thanked him as he put it to his lips and then couldn't make himself stop drinking as he moaned greater thanks that flowed out of the burst of pure flavor and refreshment.

"Come on upstairs and take a load off." Noah waved for Barney to follow as he started up the beautiful staircase to the balcony.

"How?" Barney managed to form the question after spotting something that brought his attention back from the refreshing drink to the surreal surroundings. There was something that looked like an electric hotplate next to the freezer and an electric lightbulb hanging from the ceiling. As Barney headed up the staircase, he caught a glimpse of another room under the balcony that had a workbench filled with glass flasks, test tubes, and various apparatuses the purpose of which he could not even pretend to guess.

"What do you mean, how?" Noah laughed while feigning an insulted air.

Barney was about to explain his overly perplexed demeanor when he summited the staircase and was overcome by the view from the balcony window. There was a slight break in the jungle canopy right at the spot Noah had placed his home and it allowed for a view straight down the mountainside all the way to the beach where the aircraft was resting. The sun was about to set and the colors radiating from the ocean below hypnotized him briefly until Noah offered him a seat.

"How what?" Noah reiterated as he motioned him to the wicker chair facing the window. Since he never expected to have to entertain guests, Noah only had one chair in any one part of the house, so he sat carefully on the window sill.

"Don't be cute with me. I interviewed the skiff pilot personally," Barney said in an accusatory tone.

"Oh, this is even more fun than I had hoped." Noah smirked, thankful he didn't have to go to the immodest lengths of describing the circumstances in which he came to live on this island.

A little over two years ago, Noah had convinced a crew member of *Darwin's Pride* to let him come along on a skiff outing in the archipelago, knowing that they would be passing near a group of islands he had his eye on for what he liked to call an "indefinite vacation." A bottle of twelve-year-old scotch had kept the little mission a secret, that is until Dr. Abus was able to out- bribe or threaten, depending on one's point of view, the pilot in question.

Noah had only a small daypack and the clothes on his back with him when they departed the ship just before sunrise that morning. He told the pilot not to worry about him no matter what happens and not to worry about getting in trouble because it was all cleared with the science officer. The ride was solemn yet peaceful. The low rumble of the engine and the gentle rocking motion of the skiff over the waves lulled Noah into a dreamlike state that caused him to think a little too clearly about what his plans were. He argued himself into a place that he had previously decided was too extreme even for him. The adrenaline rush coming from what he was about to do contrasted with the peace of the morning sea and the hypnotic sounds and motion of the skiff, made for an overly confident and rash split-second decision. As the skiff passed within a kilometer of the island he now calls home, he stood up, dropped his pack, and stripped down completely. The skiff pilot turned to ask how much further he wanted to go just in time to see a flash of white as Noah hurled his naked body over the side of the fast-moving boat. Of course, the pilot immediately cut the engines and leaned hard to port as if going back to pick up a downed water skier. Noah waved him off and yelled to him that he was okay, telling him that it was all part of a science experiment. He told him not to worry about picking him up, that he had made other arrangements, which was the closest thing to a lie he had said during this whole endeavor for he had only made arrangements with himself. Self-reliance, self-sufficiency—these were his arrangements. The scientific experiment part was true. He had always wanted to test himself to see if he could survive in the wild without so much as a match or even a stitch of clothing from the civilized world. He was now officially a rat in a maze of his own making although the long swim in the rough surf at times made him feel more like a gerbil in a wheel. After spending a good part of the day fighting currents and trying not to think of sharks, the swim finally ended as the sea gave birth to the newest member of the island ecosystem. Noah McAdams was deposited onto the wet sand in the fetal position and he gasped for the breath of a new life away from the world and the mistakes of the past. But even there, at the beginning of a new life, he could not block out the regrets that surfaced as memories of her. She was the only face that flashed before his eyes as he hit the surface of the water not knowing if he would ever come up for air again.

"Come on now!" Barney said, snapping Noah out of his brief melancholy. "'He went into the sea naked as the day he was born . . .' those were his exact words as I recall. Where did you get all of these amenities? Electricity? Ice? Iron? Glass? You barely had a thing in your pack as it was and you left that on the boat! The pilot said he opened it to find nothing but a stainless-steel canteen, a knife, a fire striker, and some nutrition bars."

Noah laughed. "Not just iron, by the way . . . carbon steel. Look, it's not some big mystery . . . where did you get all of the things you have back in your so-called civilized world? Someone, somewhere, took something out of the ground and made it into something useful."

"A good many someones!" Barney replied in disbelief.

"Well, I have all of those someones who came before me to thank for everything you see here."

"You mean there were people on this island before you?" Barney asked, slightly confused.

"No," Noah blurted, actually offended this time. "I'm talking about Pythagoras, Archimedes, Newton, Einstein, Edison, Tesla . . . need I go on? I have had the accumulated knowledge of these great men available to me all of my life, as we all have . . . I just happened to pay attention in class and value the importance of understanding how and why, as much as possible, the world works. Perhaps I discovered and invented a few things of my own along the way but that is neither here nor there. Isn't that why you're . . ." Noah paused and rephrased what he was about to say. "Look, Barney . . . I know why you're here and you know how I feel . . ."

Barney cut him off before he had a chance to go down the "out of the question" line of conversation. "Noah, just hear me out, please."

"First things first," Noah said, changing the subject. "I don't suppose that when our nice little visit is over that you'll fly away from here and leave me to live my life as I see fit, will you?"

"Now that wouldn't give me any leverage in our little game of chess, would it?" Barney smiled, knowing he had Noah in a corner. At the very least he could mention Noah's presence on the island to the authorities and his new life here would be over. Worst case, he could have his security detail take Noah into custody under his own authority. They were good friends, however, and Barney wanted to do everything possible to make this a "win, win" situation.

"So where do we go from here?" Noah sighed as if this revelation was a heavy weight on his chest forcing the breath of this new life out of him.

"Why don't you come back to the capital with me and we'll take as much time as we need to hammer this all out. We don't need to go into any details right now. You don't have any other pressing appointments, do you?" Barney joked and they both laughed, lightening the mood.

"Well I do have a 5:00 a.m. with a certain fish that keeps eluding my spear, but I guess he will have to be eaten by some other carnivore." They both laughed again. "It's starting to get dark. I guess that, if I have no other choice, uh . . . we better get going."

Noah stood up and took Barney's empty glass from him as if he were going to do the dishes. Once they got downstairs, he realized the futility of washing glasses that were never going to be used again, so he placed them on the table and tried not to be sentimental about leaving everything he had built here. After all, he had built all of this from nothing and he could do it again if he had to. No sense in being attached to it.

He grabbed a little jar from next to the sink and headed out the door. "I'm going to wash up before we head out, if you don't mind?"

"Please," Barney said, trying not to sound as if he was agreeing with Noah's obvious need for a shower.

"Sorry, I was fishing just before you came . . . then I fell asleep in the hammock . . . well, then I was so rudely awakened . . . I didn't get a chance to clean up." Noah actually did keep quite clean most of the time, even though there was no one else around to care. Taking a shower in the waterfall was one of his favorite pastimes and he liked to experiment with different botanicals and oils for making soaps and shampoos. It seemed silly and not exactly manly, but it was one thing that helped him to feel civilized.

"There's something else I want to show you before we take off." Noah led Barney toward the waterfall.

Barney couldn't help but wonder if Noah was suddenly going to bolt into the jungle, and it was this thought that was causing the secret eye contact with his security chief, but what he saw once they got to the waterfall completely took his mind off of anything but Noah's genius. Behind the waterfall there was a cave with a huge waterwheel driving a long shaft that extended over to a gearbox against the cliff wall toward the house. Noah had first used this to turn a saw blade that he used to mill the lumber he needed for building the house, but once he had mined enough lodestone and copper to make an electric generator, he turned it into a power plant for running the freezer, the lights, and the hot plate.

"I'm sorry . . . but again . . . how did you accomplish all of this on your own?" Barney gasped.

"Well, as soon as I had the essentials covered—water, shelter, food, and fire—all I had was time on my hands. You know me, I've always felt right at home in the jungle . . . luckily for you," Noah said, trying to gain a little leverage of his own in their little game of chess.

He was never comfortable with reminding people of their indebtedness to him, but the fact that he had saved Barney's life was the only currency he had at this point. Barney was uncharacteristically quiet, so Noah continued, a little embarrassed to have sunk to that level and to be blowing his own horn about how he did all this.

"It didn't take me long to hone the necessary skills needed to feed myself here, so I concentrated on coming up with ways of preserving food so that hunting, fishing, and gathering didn't have to be daily events. After that, I concentrated on acquiring tools that would make every task easier. This island is overflowing with natural resources that are readily available and near the surface. That's why I chose it and frankly, that's why the government has made it off-limits. Since I was not preoccupied with trying to escape the island like most people would be, I devoted myself to the task of finding and refining those resources. Once I found enough iron ore to refine, I built a furnace and bellows capable of generating the necessary temperatures. That construction not only gave me the ability to make iron tools, but it also gave me the ability to blow glass and cure pottery. I simply concentrated on making tools that make other tools possible and it's an exponential journey really. Every tool you make makes the next tool possible and before you know it, you're accomplishing impossible tasks. What's the old saying? 'Give me a lever long enough and I'll move the world'? It was the discovery of lodestone that really rocketed me into the modern age. I was quite pleased when I found enough to construct an electric generator. The compressor for the freezer took me a while, but I finally managed it."

Noah went on and on while he took a quick shower and continued as they went back to the house so he could get dressed and grab the few things he wanted to take with him. He went on about his discoveries among the flora and fauna of the island and about how some of the extracts could benefit mankind and they reminisced about the days when they both worked for ACTICORP, Noah as a field researcher and Barnard as a project administrator.

The two had previously worked as a team to bring many of Noah's discoveries to market as useful technologies, so it didn't surprise Barney that Noah would discover things that no one else had among the plants and animals here. That was how he had made a living for all those years before he left the jungle for the university. It was in fact, as Noah was trying to ask previously, why Barney was here, why he was seeking *the* Dr. Noah McAdams.

It wasn't long before Noah was running out of words. He had talked more this day than he had in two years. At first he couldn't stop himself, but now it had all become exhausting. It had become very dark and Noah had switched on the overhead light so he could find the notes he wanted to bring with him. He didn't want to take much, just the notes of his new discoveries and some small objects that accompanied them, the small stringed instrument he had made that resembled a charango from the Andes region and his favorite knife. He was now dressed in long pants and a linen-like shirt and his hair was pulled back in a ponytail. He was a far cry from the ape-man that Barney had first encountered on the beach. He reached up in the cupboard and retrieved a homemade lightbulb which he then carefully pressed down into the opening of a sort of Baghdad battery he had made from pottery, copper, and acid. As he pressed it down, it came to life with a surprisingly strong glow.

"Let's go . . . we've already burned all the daylight," Noah said with a smile that was a little forced. He came here for a reason and he didn't like being forced to leave, but more than that, he didn't like being forced to have to face why he came here, or at least one particular reason why. Her face flashed to the front of his mind for a second as he was pondering the whole situation, but in his calculating way he quickly refocused on the task at hand. He shoved his few belongings in a burlap-looking knapsack and led Barney down the steps, hitting the light switch on the way out.

He started toward the trail to the beach and then spun around suddenly, "Almost forgot . . . better let the chickens out." Barney followed him around the house to find several bamboo cages. "They kept chewing through the bars when I first put them in there, but I finally found a plant extract to coat the bamboo with that keeps them from chewing on it."

"I wasn't aware that chickens could . . . chew," Barney said surprised that he would ever have the opportunity to utter that sentence.

"These can." As Noah held the light up over the first cage in order to open the door, several furry little creatures scurried into view. Barney wasn't sure exactly what they were, they seemed to be the local version of a guinea pig—not much more than rats really, but he was afraid to ask why he had them caged.

"Chickens, eh?" Barney said under his breath as he danced instinctively to keep them from going up his pant leg as they scurried into the jungle.

Noah smiled uncontrollably. He had forgotten how much fun it was to watch Barney pretend to be an experienced bush-man while squirming like a little girl. It was because Noah was the only one on earth who had ever experienced this side of the otherwise respectable Palace Appointee that he could get away with calling him Barney.

"Well, you know what they say . . . they taste like chicken." Noah laughed, more at Barney's dancing than at his own joke.

After regaining his composure and freeing the rest of the rodents, Noah headed back toward the waterfall, mostly out of habit. He always disengaged the waterwheel when going on an exploratory hike around the island and he was still holding out hope that Barney would relent and allow him to come back here when all was said and done, so he didn't want the equipment to wear out.

"Hold this for a second." Noah handed Barney the home-made lantern and slid behind the gearbox. He grabbed a long lever with both hands and yanked it with all his weight. There was a loud clank and then nothing but the sound of the waterfall. It was strange how one couldn't detect the whirring of the generator beneath the sound of the waterfall until it was noticeably absent. The whole compound was similar in its intimacy with the natural surroundings. Even though the house had a beautiful view of the ocean, the opposite was not true. Even the beach house was camouflaged enough to keep anyone from seeing it from more than 100 meters. If it were not for Noah's fresh footprints in the sand, the aircraft pilot would never have seen it.

"Well, that's it." Noah sighed. The light from the lantern was briefly eclipsed by the long handle of the lever as Noah passed through the narrow space behind the gear box. It resembled a flaming sword and at that moment he felt as if he were passing out of the very gates of Eden. He received the lantern back from Barney as if they were passing the torch for the next leg of the journey, then he headed down the mountainside without saying another word and without looking back. Noah was strangely grateful for the darkness, especially as they lifted off and flew over the island. Even darkness serves its purpose . . . Dr. Noah McAdams could no longer hide from his.

CHAPTER THREE

"Ground duty! After all I sacrificed to get on the Project." He couldn't help but say it out loud even though there was no one else in the cockpit, or for hundreds of miles for that matter, to hear him bemoan his overactive sense of quality and safety. "I should have kept my mouth shut."

Yafeu Agymah Amadi had spent the last several years cycling through tours of construction duty on the engineering section of *Epoch Utopia* or "The Great Tower in the Sky" as he called it. He named it that on his first shuttle ride to the site to report for duty. As the shuttle approached, they were coming toward it at such an angle as to make it appear as if it were a great tower growing right out of the Earth's horizon. He had never seen anything like it and even without the three outer sections attached, it was the largest construction ever built by man. The backdrop of space did not do it justice for there was nothing to compare it to. It seemed to grow in the window for hours even though it was a forty-five-minute flight and it was difficult to look straight at it because of the reflected sunlight that was unencumbered by the atmosphere at that altitude. It wasn't until the window was completely filled with the great ship that he spotted another shuttle halfway between them and their destination that appeared like a bug on the window. It was so large that if it had been constructed on the surface of the Earth the engineers would have had to compensate for the curvature of the Earth.

Yafeu's sense of self was altered that day as he was confronted with a reality that was larger than himself, larger than his family, his community, and frankly his worldview. It was almost a spiritual experience. He was only a Signal Path Technician on the Project, but he believed so much in what he was doing that his zeal often landed him in trouble with peers and even with his superiors who were less enthusiastic than he. After several instances of his concerns being ignored by his immediate supervisor, he made the mistake of trying to talk to the site engineer himself.

Yafeu was not one to complain under his breath that the engineers didn't know what they were doing, like so many of the other technicians. He realized he was just a technician and he didn't have the advantage of access to the big picture, but he was also convinced that the engineers could benefit greatly from the hands-on experience of the technicians. He had several ideas of how to standardize the systems he was installing and he had several concerns about potential sub-system failures and even safety concerns. The other technicians only cared about their little task-oriented world and some of them took shortcuts that could actually cause more work in the long run. They just cared about logging their assignments as complete to make their own numbers look good. They didn't care that often times another technician would have to be assigned to come behind them and fix their mess.

Time was of utmost importance to those in charge because the Palace had placed inhuman demands and deadlines on them. Nothing of this scale had ever been attempted before, so that meant that their benchmarking process was little more than a shot in the dark. Yafeu had heard a quote once, he was not sure who it was from, but he made it a life motto: "If you don't have time to do it right, when will you have time to do it over?" He thought that if he could just reach the right person with enough authority he was certain that he could convince him or her to implement his ideas with promises of overall time savings and higher quality. He was even prepared to chart out the cost savings that are inherent to doing things right the first time, not that cost seemed to be an issue for the Palace, but old habits of microeconomics are hard to break. Yafeu had worked for a communications company in what was still called the private sector where costs meant something because there was still the illusion of competition between companies for market share. That was illusion only. In reality, the different companies were nothing more than semi-separate divisions of the government. The Administration had access to and control over all of the assets and so-called profits of all of the companies, so the big picture was that the sky was the limit, literally in this case. The Palace had all of the resources of the world, human and otherwise, at its disposal as well as the previously untapped resources of the near solar system.

As can be imagined, all of this enthusiasm and extra effort did not endear Yafeu to the other techs and since his supervisor was not much more than a glorified tech, he often tried his patience as well. The supervisor was more concerned with Yafeu hurting his log numbers by spending more time on each job than the other techs than he was with listening to any of his free thinking and grandiose ideas. He wasn't concerned with rework because that was someone else's logbook. That kind of short-sightedness often leads to failure and sometimes disaster.

Well at least that failure would not be on his watch. That was the only solace he had concerning his career at this point. He had worked very hard to qualify for not only the construction team but for crew status, and his hopes concerning that seemed to be falling as quickly as the altimeter on the utility craft he was now assigned to. The craft suddenly broke through the light cloud cover and the familiar sight of the lush West African coast burst into view. He was briefly distracted by the comforting sight of home, but he only had a few minutes to take it in before he would have to start the landing sequence. He forced his attention back into the cockpit and rechecked his repair assignment to get his bearings. He had spotted the main communications array for the region while looking out the window and instinctively knew from the failure data which direction he would have to head from there to find the problem. He sighed as he began the landing sequence and felt the effects of the changes in g-forces. He couldn't seem to shake the similar feeling of backward momentum stemming from his recent demotion.

Ground duty was not simply managing the signals being beamed to the project site, but it also meant that he would be on loan to the regional communications utility. The duty he had pulled this day had nothing to do with the Project at all which made him feel all the more the backward forces being applied to his career. He was on a repair call to a remote village that was having intermittent connection issues with the main network. Not only was he banned to the furthest reaches of the Earth where nothing new and exciting was happening, but he was being sent on the communications version of a wild goose chase as well.

Intermittent problems are the bane of a technician's existence because the chances of being at the right place at the right time to run the right test to find the cause of the problem are slim to none. Evidence of the futility placed before him was found in the repair records of the assignment. This case has already had three technicians dispatched on it, some of them more than once. Yafeu mined deeper into the repair log database to find the notes from the previous technicians. After reading all of the notes and trouble reports and reviewing the previous test results, he found something conspicuously absent among the data. There was never a test taken with a direct connection at the local HUB. There were notes saying that they performed tests at that site, but no data logs were ever created, which told Yafeu one of two things: either there is a larger problem with data tracking on the system, or they lied about performing the tests. After what he has been through, neither option would surprise him, but he knew many technicians and their tendencies toward shortcuts, so he was leaning toward the latter.

Normally, Yafeu would do things by the book and go to the end user point first—where the trouble was being reported—but with this revelation he thought he would gamble and head to the HUB first. In his mind, this was not a shortcut but good troubleshooting. He reached out in front of him and touched the destination area on the utility craft console screen. He downloaded the coordinates of the HUB from the assignment log and hit the "update destination" control. The craft shuddered momentarily and banked slightly until it achieved its new vector then an ambiguous voice said, "Estimated time to arrival: five minutes." He was tempted to lose himself in thought for the next five minutes, but he knew if he did he would just become angry again, so he got up from the pilot seat and slipped back into the cargo area to do a quick inventory of things he needed for the job.

That particular distraction was short-lived, however, as a new one took its place. Yafeu spun around and shot back into the cockpit as a loud warning alarm sounded. He gave the computer a voice command to give him the details of the situation as he sat back down in the pilot seat. It seemed that the location of the HUB was so remote that the standard landing platform next to it had been overgrown by the thick brush. The computer was not capable of landing the craft under those circumstances without a warning override from the pilot. Yafeu did one better and simply took manual control of the craft. He had grown up in this region and this wasn't the first time he had to land in the brush. He knew what he needed to avoid and what he could simply crush on his way down. He doubted that the computer would be able to make those kinds of judgments. The proximity alarm came on just before the sound of branches was heard scraping the side of the craft and then snapping as their feeble attempt to keep the technological world out was thwarted. Yafeu impatiently yelled a voice command at the computer to silence the alarms and then eased the craft down onto the overgrown pad with a slight bump and a sudden stop.

Luckily the cargo door slid sideways, otherwise he would have been trapped in the vehicle by the offending brush. Yafeu always kept a machete in his craft for just such an occasion. He grabbed up his tool belt, swung it over his shoulder, and started hacking his way through to the two-meter-high metal box that was the reason for his reluctant expedition. It took him a minute to even see which direction he needed to head, but after several minutes he found himself at the HUB and clearing space to open the doors. He took out his locking tool and tapped loudly several times on the door and the top of the box. The reason for doing this became obvious as he unlocked the handle and gingerly opened the door to the big box. He was just barely able to sense movement inside as the door was slightly cracked open then he jumped back instinctively as he flung the door wide. There was an angry hiss and a violent writhing as the occupant of the convenient shelter was surprised by his uninvited guest.

"Well, I guess we know why no one has taken a test from here!" Yafeu almost yelled as he couldn't overcome the adrenaline coursing through his body. "Oooh, you're an angry one. Aren't you? And dangerous too!" he said as the serpent tried to take a swipe at him. "Well, I'm not afraid of you!" Yafeu had noticed from their tech IDs that none of the other techs dispatched on this trouble were from this region. His suspicions had just been confirmed that the others had found something that they didn't want to deal with at the site and simply closed out their assignment tickets with a "No Trouble Found," knowing that they could get away with it since the trouble was intermittent. He was hoping it was going to be something technical, but the fact that none of them were from the region pointed to a biological infestation of some sort. "Those city boys usually just close it back up and fly away whenever they find something squirming around in there," he said in a disgusted tone under his breath.

Yafeu jogged back to the vehicle while trying to keep a fix on the location of his opponent at all times. He quickly grabbed an extension pole and a roll of small cable. He made a quick loop with the cable and attached it to the end of the pole and marched back to the box holding the contraption like a spear. There were a variety of deadly snake species in that area and Yafeu was not taking any chances with this one, especially considering the confined space. It was coiled up among what looked like a rat's nest of fiber-optic cables of varying colors and sizes. Misidentification was a deadly game and was almost certain in this case, so there was no way he was going to stick his hand in there. He gently moved the pole into place, giving the snake something to strike at. As the snake struck, Yafeu just turned his wrist over, laying the top side of the loop behind him. Unwittingly, the snake had just struck himself into a hangman's noose. All Yafeu had to do now was gently pull the loop taut and that was that. He tightened it enough to keep it from escaping but not enough to hurt it. He didn't have anything against it, it was just being what it was—a snake. He just didn't want it to go back in there, which they had a tendency to do. It was a readymade hideout for a snake that feels threatened. Why wouldn't it slither right back in there once freed? It was this thought process that had Yafeu reaching for his machete, but as he pulled its entire meter-and-a-half length clear, he was confident that he had a good enough grip on it to keep it captive until he could make his repairs and permanently seal the box so it couldn't return. He wanted to avoid killing it if he could. He had seen enough death in his lifetime.

That was one of the reasons why he wanted a place on the crew so badly. He wanted to leave behind the memories of a childhood of death brought on by, what seemed to be at the time, endless, brutal regime change. When the Supreme Ruler finally took control, the bloodshed ended because none of the local warlords were any match for his unimpeded global power. He put everyone in the region to work building the very network he was repairing today. The Babel Resurgence Project was the ultimate expression of that newfound hope to Yafeu. He longed to leave death behind and begin life anew among the stars.

Yafeu tied off the free end of the cable and gently set the pole down well away from the HUB then he cautiously shined his utility light in and behind the coils of fiber optics to make sure that there were no other surprises waiting for him. After a minute or so he was satisfied and he began his repairs. He connected his field computer to the equipment and ran the tests that everyone else had left undone only to find that the very reason they had left the tests undone was the source of the trouble. The snake had repeatedly bedded down on top of the fiber-optic bundles and, in doing so, it was causing violation of the bend radius of the fiber optics. If the snake was home, you had signal trouble; if he wasn't, you may not and your trouble would not often be in the same place. Yafeu was sure that if he cross-referenced this trouble ticket assignment with others in the area he would find that many of the local villages were having similar problems because they were all fed from this HUB. If it were up to him, he would upgrade the whole system with a hard splice system that minimized coiled fiber, but that would take about a week for one technician and he knew for a fact that that would not fly with his boss. The best he could do here would be to replace some of the oldest fiber with the newer higher grade fiber which was not quite as susceptible to bend radius violation.

After replacing the most worn fiber, he sealed even the slightest opening in the metal box with a foam that dries as hard as concrete and then he sprayed the box, inside and out, with an industrial-strength pest repellant. He closed the doors with a slam that made the snake writhe with an explosion of second wind energy in a futile attempt to flee. He locked the box down tight with the locking tool and then carefully picked up the extension pole. He made sure that he positioned himself between the snake and the vehicle just in case he had to flee himself once he let the snake go. He untied the loose end of the cable and gently let the snake down and gave it some slack. The snake hit the ground and exploded off in the direction of the HUB just as Yafeu had suspected.

"Good luck try'n ta get in there," he said with a sly smile. As soon as the snake was close enough to get the slightest sense of the repellant, it shot back in the completely opposite direction which happened to be straight for Yafeu. His sly smile turned to a split-second expression of horror and before he could get his wits about him, he found himself high-stepping toward the vehicle. He jumped in the open cargo door with a burst of laughter the likes of which he hadn't let fly since the days he used to tease his little brother to the breaking point then run away in laughter as his brother chased him with a stick. As that memory came flooding over him, his laughter gave way to a solemn sigh and he whispered, "Goodbye, brother" as he looked through the closing door at the enraged snake.

It was a short flight to the village that was having the signal troubles. He had to register a test from that location in order to log the job as closed, so there was no avoiding a journey into his past. He had actually been to this village several times before. It was a stopping-off point for several of the refugee migrations he had been a part of as a child. He was just now starting to realize that part of the angry mood he had been in all day was stemming from seeing the name of this village on his work order this morning and not simply from his recent demotion.

He set down near the community access portal in the center of the village to great curiosity from the villagers. They came out of the woodwork to see what the noise was and they smiled with excitement when they saw that it was a utility vehicle in hopes that their connection to the outside world might be reestablished. This was quite a commotion for the small village. They didn't often see craft landing in the village. There was a shuttle stop about two kilometers outside of town, but that was the extent of the traffic in the area normally. The villagers had the ability to get to the city on the shuttle, but many of them never really felt the need since there was also a supply depot at the shuttle stop, and now that their network connection was being repaired, they had access to the entire world, virtually.

The children got the finest education while seated around the community access portal. It was an education riddled with government propaganda but a good education nonetheless. Some of these children may, like Yafeu, even end up working in space some day. This was the genius plan of the Supreme Ruler. His method of control was not in dumbing down education to ensure that there were ignorant masses like so many dictators had done before him. He wanted everyone to show their potential so that he could use the cumulative potential of all of mankind for his purposes. He still needed to include propaganda in the education system to shape their worldview at a young age. He found that this made it much easier to get people to do what he wanted them to when they were older while at the same time making them think that it was their own idea to do the very things that he was grooming them for. He had created, through his brightest and closest advisors, a filter system for accessing the world network that would identify people's aptitudes and interests and would continue to customize their individual connection by restricting access to information and ideas that did not forward his agenda for them. They didn't even know. They thought that they had free access to the entire world of knowledge while all along they were being led down a path that was chosen for them by the Supreme Ruler for his own purposes because of their abilities.

The Ruler started network projects all around the world, even in the most remote areas, for it was his intention to harness the potential of all of mankind. As soon as he gained control of a region, he immediately put the people to work on the network and gave them access to it. He was a hero to all by bringing peace and stability, jobs and access to a larger world that many didn't even know existed. It was a form of slavery that the world had never known, one where most of the slaves thought they were free. The Ruler dealt with those who had caught on to the scheme and insisted on what he saw as the outdated idea of individual liberty and self-determination, but he rarely had the need. He was so in control of information that even those who had caught on could be deceived by his constant manipulation of information and counter-intelligence. Besides, most people were content with their place in life under his regime because by default they were able to fulfill their potential. Some of those who didn't have much potential were doomed to the mundane tasks that had not yet been automated somehow, but most of them were simply housed and fed like cattle, like breeding stock from which the next Mozart or Einstein might mysteriously appear. He was insightful enough to understand that the human genome is unpredictable and immeasurably powerful. He felt he needed to monitor everyone, no matter what their pedigree, not that he didn't have advanced genetic engineering programs and social engineering programs—the most important of which was the future population of *Epoch Utopia*—but he didn't want to take any chances that might cause him to miss that one person that may make that one breakthrough that would catapult him into eternal godhood.

Yafeu sheepishly slid through the gaggle of small children circled around the cylindrical network portal in the center of the village square. He didn't like being the center of attention, but there was absolutely no avoiding it. It helped that it looked as if they were happy to see him, but he was still embarrassed to have everyone in the whole village staring at him. Often when a technician arrived at a repair location the people would be very ungrateful and hold them personally responsible for all of their problems as if they caused them instead of the truth, that they're there to fix them. This was a refreshing change but still uncomfortable.

"Excuse me, please. I just have a few tests to perform, then I'll be out of your way." He directed his comment mostly toward the children's instructor but loudly enough that the people in the crowd that had gathered could hear.

"No problem. We were hoping that you would come before the Supreme Ruler's speech," the instructor said with an excited yet concerned look that had an "it's about time . . . it's about to start" air to it. "We were in the middle of our lesson earlier and the whole village lost connection. Is that going to happen during the speech?"

"No, sorry, that was me. I had to disconnect you briefly at another location to fix your problem once and for all."

"Are you sure about that?" came from an anonymous voice in the crowd and before Yafeu had a chance to answer, someone else chimed in. "We've been having this problem for quite a while now and no one else seemed to be able to fix it."

There was a chorus of agreement among the villagers that Yafeu had to overcome with his confident answer. "I'm absolutely sure that that particular problem won't be returning."

It may have been the picture in his head he had of the enraged snake fleeing his former home that caused him to speak in such a way, but whatever it was, he spoke with such authority that the crowd believed in him, even after having heard the same message over and over again from the other technicians, with no results.

"I'll have the speech on for you in just a minute or so." He unlocked the back of the metal cylinder with military speed and precision and then made his field computer seem to appear out of nowhere with one hand while connecting the test lead to the port with the other. He stood conspicuously in silence with all eyes on him while the test was running its course. The status bar on the small screen seemed to mock him as it slowly grew like the tension in the air caused by the impatience of an entire village.

In the silence, his mind wandered into a whole inner dialogue about how with all of the technology that exists now . . . *one would think that they would give us field computers and test software that could do the job faster than this. After all, the signals move at near the speed of light . . . do you know how much time that would save us? . . . I could be on my way to see my wife and kids . . .* His thoughts were soon interrupted by the "Test Complete" indicator that was shortly followed by the "Test Successful" indicator. He was very pleased to see the latter because there were seemingly endless reasons why a test could fail and he really didn't want to do any troubleshooting in front of the whole village. He also wanted to get out of there before he had the chance to notice things in his surroundings that would dredge up the past. This was one of the last places he saw his little brother alive, and though he liked to think about his brother, he couldn't stand to think about the massacre that stole that precious innocent child from him. It happened not far from here and it has taken all Yafeu's strength to focus on the task at hand long enough to get the job done and leave this place behind once again.

Yafeu snatched the test lead out of the portal, holstered his field computer, and slammed the door shut with a confident finality. He came around to the front of the portal and said, "Let me get the speech up for you." He brought up the

World News Network menu and checked the lead story link. "Oh, it looks like it has already started . . ." He had to raise his voice over the unhappy crowed to finish his statement. "Let me start it from the beginning for you. It will reset to real time once the speech is finished." Suddenly a ghostly figure appeared in their midst and, though Yafeu had chosen the life-size scale on the holographic emitter, the man seemed to tower over everyone in the crowd. They all instinctively shrunk back a few steps and then seemed to go into a trance as he started to speak.

"Today . . . we make history!" The crowd, as always, went wild, both at the steps of the Palace and around the world where most were watching in the same manner as this little village. The striking figure in the hologram had to pause for what seemed like minutes, but even in his silence he was convincing and inspiring. The roar soon turned to a rumble and he continued to move the crowd forward with his agenda for the occasion. "Today we make history . . . you and I and all who bear the name Human . . . today . . . we make history . . . for . . ." Again, the Supreme Ruler was interrupted by the roaring ocean of praise forcing its way up the steps of the Palace like a human tidal wave crashing at his feet. He hadn't even yet told them why they were making history, but that didn't matter to many of them. They were so conditioned, almost programmed by his propaganda and his individual information filter software, that every word from his mouth was like gold to them. His silence again hypnotized them into submission and he continued, ". . . for, after the events of today, it is a foregone conclusion that our name will be known . . . THROUGHOUT THE UNIVERSE!" As his speech turned to a charismatic scream, the people could no longer control themselves. There was such elation that the security teams had to take some unwitting participants down just to keep the crowd from spilling up the Palace steps. They weren't thinking ahead about what this plan might mean for them or their family or people they know, they were just overcome by an intangible, grandiose, utopian idea, the emotion of which was the only thing that mattered.

As Noah watched from the aircraft, he was disgusted by the behavior of the mind-numbed masses. Such behavior was so foreign to him. He couldn't understand it. The Ruler had not even told them anything of substance yet and they acted as if he had just granted them eternal life. It was quite unsettling to him. The Supreme Ruler—the way the world reacted to him and the Babel Resurgence Project itself—it all seemed askew somehow, like a dark force had somehow taken history and bent it in an effort to derail the way things were suppose to be in favor of this new, dark track. This feeling was the other reason Noah had decided to check out from society two years ago. Now he was not only being forced back into the madness but he was being coerced into forwarding the agenda of this madman. It was almost more than he could handle for this to be his first taste of civilization after being away from it all for so long, but he managed to camouflage his disgust with the slight feelings of airsickness that he was feeling. He knew he was in deep already and, though he trusted Barney, he didn't want to rock the boat with an emotional tirade against the very person that granted Dr. Abus his power and prestige. So, in his calculated way, Noah took a deep breath and refocused on the speech.

"Today we make history . . . today the combined efforts of mankind have culminated in the glorious creation of a vessel that will carry the light of humanity to the very heart of the universe . . ." This time the leader didn't stop for the crowd; he overpowered them with a voice that came from a deep, dark place, a voice that flattered and accused all at the same time. ". . . no longer will we be an infinitesimal and inconsequential spec in the vastness of space, but we will be known . . . we will have a great and glorious name among the stars! We have gathered together as one on this small planet to accomplish all that we have pleased to and we will grow . . . as one . . . we will spread across the universe . . . as one . . . Today! WE MAKE HISTORY!" With this, he paused again, artfully concluding by willing them into submission with his insanity concealed in charismatic optimism. ". . . from this day on, we will progressively strive, with all that we are, to find man at the center of the universe!"

As the crowd continued to roar, the overwhelming noise morphed into a single coherent chant and the people started to sway back and forth, "Today! We make history! Today . . ." Finally the World News Network anchor came back up on the viewer.

"And there you have it, the Supreme Ruler christening the vessel which has become known to many as the hope of humanity with a very inspiring speech, once again uniting the entire world. Let's go now to the science desk for an update on the reason for today's speech. Dr. Sorenson?"

"Thank you, Bob. Today, in case you weren't paying attention, we have made history. The *Interpreter One* computer that was launched a few days ago has now been successfully integrated into the superstructure of *Epoch Utopia* and, as these live shots from orbit will show, the vessel has now come to life as the three outer sections rotate effortlessly around the long, cylindrical, engineering section that runs like an axle through their hubs." He used a pointing device as a professor would as he continued to explain the vessel to those watching. "The living areas of the vessel are held out from the hubs by the spokes of these giant wheels. There are six of them here—it may look as if there are only four—but if you watch carefully you will see that the center section, IUPATER, is twice the size—or more precisely—twice the mass of either of the other sections by themselves. It is rotating the opposite direction of the other two so that what looks like two thicker wheels holding the middle section is really four wheels—two holding the center section rotating one direction and two holding the ends of the other sections rotating in the opposite direction. The reason for the rotation itself is to provide a centripetal force in the living areas that simulates approximately one G of gravity. The reason for the opposite rotations is to give the vessel itself a net zero axial inertia. None of this would be possible without the *Interpreter One* constantly, well . . . interpreting between the computers on the four different sections of the vessel. Being built by four different cultures, these computers in a very real sense speak four different languages, and not only do the computers speak different languages but so do all of the people involved in the Project. Once the vessel leaves Earth's orbit and is no longer in range of the world network, the *Interpreter One* will also do the translation that is taken for granted here. When was the last time that you thought about the fact that I am hearing you in my language and you are hearing me in yours, Bob?"

"Not since before my implant, Doctor." They both laughed and Dr. Sorenson continued to explain how the activation of the *Interpreter One* had gone off without a hitch, assuring everyone that any glitches so far were minor and that the Project was well on schedule.

That was too much for Dr. Abus because he knew the reality of the glitches and the schedule so he switched off the viewer. He sensed that it was too much stimulus for Noah as well, so he reassured him that they would be landing soon. "We have a lot to talk about and you have a lot to catch up on, but no need to do it all in one sitting."

Noah nodded with a look of relief and thanked his old friend. They were both content to sit in silence for the short remainder of the journey, and before he knew it Noah found himself looking down on the grand capital of the world, the ancient city between the rivers. The craft landed gracefully on a private pad just outside Abus's office in the Palace complex. There was a small entourage of staff members awaiting their arrival, and Abus scanned them impatiently as he debarked.

"Where's Lisa?" he shouted over the dying engines to the first staff member that reached him.

"She told me she had to cover for you over at the cabinet meeting and gave me your briefing update." The staffer handed him an electronic pad and stepped out of his way knowing that he might get trampled otherwise.

"Lisa?" Noah asked quietly as they cleared the range of the engine noise.

"My assistant, well, more like my prime minister," Abus said with a concerned look. "It is very unlike her not to be here when I land."

"Dr. McAdams?" another staffer inserted respectfully.

"Yes," Noah answered, a little overwhelmed by the flurry of human activity around them.

"When you are ready, there is a transport waiting to take you to your apartment," the staffer said while making eye contact with Dr. Abus.

Dr. Abus nodded and said. "Go ahead, Noah, you must want to clean up and rest a little. We'll continue tomorrow."

"What I really want is a good cup of Ethiopian coffee and some Swiss chocolate!" Noah said with a smile but in a way that could not be mistaken for a joke.

"It's waiting for you in your apartment, Doctor, along with a nice bottle of scotch," the staffer said without missing a beat.

Noah nodded at Barney and started off behind the staffer trying not to think about how they knew his every whim and trying not to notice the security detail following him.

"Get some rest!" Barney yelled out after him. "You've got a new life ahead of you!"

After Noah was out of sight, Dr. Abus turned to his security chief and ordered, "No one knows he is here . . . he talks to no one, sees no one . . . not until we finish our conversation . . . you got that?"

"Yes, sir. It's under control," the Chief said respectfully as he flashed the palm of his hand holding the new earpiece meant for Dr. Noah McAdams.

CHAPTER FOUR

The noise was still almost unbearable in the Palace courtyard long after he had left the podium. His staff was watching him intently for any indications of whether or not he intended to grace the people with an encore as he came through the opulent four-meter-high double doors leading to the terrace where he had just finished his speech. There would be no such grace given today. He continued on past his usual reemergence queue, which caused a fury of activity among those who were expected to read his mind as they tried to stay one step ahead of his every whim.

"The Cabinet has convened in the royal council chamber and are patiently awaiting your arrival, Your Majesty," said a small, dark man in a whispery voice that was not intended to be quiet, just cautiously respectful. There was no actual response from the ruler, for he was responded to, not the other way around. He simply continued walking and everyone around him was left to assume that he was headed directly to the next agenda item for the day which was the cabinet meeting of which he was so artfully reminded. One never told the Supreme Ruler where he was to go or what he was to do; one stated the reality of the moment which was prepared for him ahead of time according to his wishes. He continued to walk past the electric Mag-Lev vehicle that routinely carried him from place to place in the immense Palace complex like a slaveless sedan chair. The vehicle slipped silently in behind the leader's entourage just in case he decided to ride, and as they cantered along trying to keep pace with his long strides, the sound of their dress shoes on the marble floors in the great hall was not unlike the sound of cavalry following a conquering king as he parades in to a new city.

His entourage was always large, but few ever really broached the barrier of his inner circle. Most in the party were simply there to take orders or relay information. When one was tasked with something that required him to leave his post, there was always another waiting in the wings to fill the void. There were only three that actually interacted with the dictator without being first acknowledged in some way. These three men were always with him and were very mysterious, even to those in the entourage. They knew them as the ones to address when wishing to interact with the Supreme Ruler and as the ones to take orders from. They had little, if any, public presence short of always being just off camera behind the Leader, and no one in the entourage even knew their first names. Even if one tried to do a network search about them, nothing would come up, no matter what clearance and credentials one had. It was as if they didn't exist or more accurately, it was as if they pre-existed the technology that recorded the history that the rest of the world knew.

The three men were being passed information by the others as they encircled the Leader, still trying to keep up with his oversized gait, and every now and then one or the other of them would relay pertinent information to him or send someone off and running in the other direction. A younger man was sent scampering on ahead in the most dignified manner one can manage while still getting out in front of such a giant. He turned a corner and burst through the doors at the end of the slightly smaller but still extravagant hall. Everyone in the room instantly knew what the interruption meant, and they quickly dispensed with the pre-meeting preparations and started to straighten their attire in whatever way appropriate until a cold chill came over each of them, in turn, according to their place in the pecking order.

"His Eminence Afzal Jamail Sargon, Supreme Ruler of Earth and the system of Sol graces you, his loyal servants and brothers in humanity, with the presence of his wisdom!" As the young, out-of-breath man announced his imminent arrival, they all stood with heads slightly bowed. Fortunately for them it was not difficult to keep one's head lower than the Ruler's because of his uncommon stature, but the slight bow was nonetheless protocol. He entered the chamber and walked around the perimeter to the far side, avoiding the sunken floor in the center where the cabinet members were standing around a large semicircle table that faced an even higher platform than the perimeter floor. Reaching the far side, he stepped up on the platform, turned, and nodded as he sat down on what can only be described as a throne. As he nodded and sat, the rest of the room followed suit until there was a room full of silent, seated statues awaiting his command to be brought back to life.

"Begin," he commanded in a tone that made one believe that it was a law of nature for people to hang on his every word. The room sprang to life with staff members passing last-minute information to the cabinet members as each member addressed the Ruler in order of standard protocol. The Three shrunk back into the shadows behind the throne, emerging every so often to whisper in the Ruler's ear or receive an unknown command.

The meeting lasted hours and after covering the state of the four economic unions, each one in turn and at length, the agenda turned to security concerns and how to maintain the illusion of a world at peace—not in those terms, of course. No one present, not even the Supreme Ruler himself, would admit that what they were doing was maintaining an illusion. Never were terms such as war or enemies used in these discussions and certainly nothing of the sort ever was allowed on the World News Network or able to be searched on the computer network. Occasionally a term such as *conflict* or *criminals* was bantered about, but to admit in a cabinet meeting that all was not well in the world was a sure way to put a target on one's back that had the inscription "place blame here," and there were very real consequences that accompanied the responsibility of such blame.

Of course, the Supreme Ruler knew very well the reality of the absence of real peace in the world between certain factions and of the reality of dissidents of his own regime. The Three kept him apprised of such things, and he personally dealt with these situations with swift and merciless finality. Everyone in the Administration knew to fear his personal attention and knew never to speak of that fear for the rest of the world was to have nothing but admiration for him. Even the Three were kept under his thumb by this fear regardless of the fact they were the creators and maintainers of the eavesdropping software that was hidden in the translation server on the world network. They could categorize and prioritize virtually every conversation on the planet, yet he was still able to exercise power over the three of them by secretly turning them on each other. He had taken an opportune moment with each of them alone to voice his concerns about the loyalty of one of the other two and followed it with flattery and a very uncharacteristic, heartfelt "You're the only one I feel I can trust . . ." Each one thought he was the only one really in the good graces and full confidence of the Ruler and happily provided intel on one or both of the others. This happiness didn't come exactly from some inner need for his approval but from the power trip that comes with the illusion of being the second most powerful person in the known universe. Any bright thoughts of attempting to become the most powerful were instantaneously snuffed out by the darkness, the deep darkness in the eye of Afzal Jamail Sargon. Even in an age of technological equalizers between men, to be in a room alone with Afzal Jamail Sargon was to be fearful. His imposing physical stature was only the frame that enhanced the horrifying picture of ruthless, morally bankrupt intellect and dark, narcissistic spirituality. With this system, he had things well under control. The cabinet ministers and other key administrators didn't know specifically about the eavesdropping program created by the Three, but they had access to the intel that it provided, when necessary. They didn't ask where it came from or how it was obtained, but they learned, each one in turn, not to speak against the character or agenda of Afzal Jamail Sargon.

After the security briefing, the meeting turned to the real reason the Ruler was there, the Babel Resurgence Project. In a very real sense the Project was the reason for everything they had already discussed as well. All of the fruit of the world economy was gathered and devoured by the Ruler's obsession. All the conflicts around the world, at some level, had as either a cause or a goal the acquisition, control, and utilization of the world's natural resources for use in the Project. It didn't stop with just the world's natural resources. The whole space program was in some way connected to the Project. Whether it was research and development of the necessary technologies needed for such an undertaking or the mining of lunar, planetary, and asteroidal materials, every effort in the space program was to eventually build, equip, populate, and launch a self-sustaining, multigenerational vessel toward, not the center of the galaxy—for that would not be ambitious enough for such a man as Afzal Jamail Sargon—but toward the center of the universe. Quite literally, the creation of a manmade, navigable planet. His creation.

It seemed insane on its face, but what higher goal could the Ruler of everything man has ever known set for himself, short of discovering God Himself? And since he didn't believe in God, per se, that was exactly what he was doing. It really was insane. His very carefully contrived public persona was convincing enough though. He was very careful to speak of the Project as a multigenerational, evolutionary arm of the human race and how that, some day, eons from now, our descendants will witness the very birthplace of all that exists because of the history-making events of the day and so on, but in private, among his closest advisors, things were much different. In reality he was obsessed with not just finding man at the center of the universe but finding himself there personally, however absurd that idea may be.

The vessel itself was designed for continuous improvement, was equipped with every type of propulsion that had yet been theorized, and populated with the brightest and most innovative minds tasked with coming up with the next theory of propulsion or teleportation or something beyond words to describe at this point. Sargon was counting on technology continuing to advance in the exponential manner that the last century had sparked. He wasn't just leaving his fate in the hands of spacecraft engineers, however; he was exploring every possibility. He had teams of experts specializing in nanotechnology for cell regeneration, bionics, artificial intelligence, quantum transportation, ESP, metaphysical exploration, and even spiritualism all working toward his goal. He even had a cryonics team available at all times in case the unthinkable happened, as a last resort, to gain more time for technology to catch up to his goal. He had advisors on these subjects that even the Three didn't know about, some of which even claimed to be in communication with other, let's just say "non-human" life forms.

As if this wasn't all enough to slake his egocentrism, the Ruler had also taken the traditional route to immortality that many potentates before him had taken. He took unto himself wife after wife after wife and procreated almost enough to fill the vessel with his own children. He was currently grooming his oldest son to take his place as ruler of Earth when he sails off into space, history, and mythology. Son or no son, there were certain things that he would only reveal to him the day of departure—like, for example, the existence of the eavesdropping program. He was unable to trust even his own son with such things. He was a student of history, and history told him that often times a king's worst enemy is his own heir. With each child born, the odds of that historical fact visiting him increased, but it wasn't something he couldn't deal with. If one son got out of line, there were plenty more waiting for their chance to prove themselves to their father.

In fact, Sargon had already started to choose candidates from his sons to rule over the colonies they would leave off along the journey. Part of the plan was to find habitable planets or moons along the way and, at least once a generation, leave a colony behind. There were several reasons for this—the most obvious of which was population control on the vessel itself. Over-population would lead to either the death of everyone or the death of the most helpless. It was not seen as a problem with the social engineering planned for the marriage and family arrangements and with the room for expansion around the outside of the great wheels of the vessel, but colonization was the built-in safety valve of population pressure. The second reason for leaving people off along the way was for backward communication of the exploits of the great explorer Afzal Jamail Sargon. Eventually people would be travelling back and forth from colony to colony and possibly even back to Earth and with them would go stories of his greatness. Possibly the biggest reason for the colonization in the Ruler's mind was that he would truly be the Ruler of the Known Universe, albeit by proxy of his progeny.

It was this colonization plan that caused Dr. Noah McAdams to be sought after and ultimately found. There seemed to be some destiny here that no amount of reluctance on his part was going to defy. Lisa was hoping that the importance of the whole subject of colonization to the Ruler and the fact that Dr. Abus was currently on an important mission regarding this would be cause for some mercy on the part of the Ruler toward Dr. Abus on account of his absence until now. She wasn't worried so much about herself and having to cover for him before the Ruler, because she knew the Doctor's schedule better than anyone . . . she composed it. She knew that he would be back in time to do the briefing himself and she knew she didn't really need to be there. She could have sent a staffer to take notes on the other members' briefings. She had her own reasons for not meeting the craft when it landed and those reasons were strong enough to cause her to risk having to brief the Supreme Ruler personally.

As the clock ticked on and it drew closer to Dr. Abus's time slot, she was, for the first time, getting a little nervous that he wasn't going to make it on time. She tried not to regret her decision as she quickly reviewed the agenda for the Doctor's briefing, but more importantly she tried not to obsess about every little thing that could possibly go wrong which was very difficult for her. She seemed to have it all together on the outside and she was highly respected and esteemed by everyone who knew her or even briefly came into contact with her, but inside she was a constant tempest of free-firing neurons working out every negative scenario to the nth degree. It often led to personal turmoil, lack of sleep, and slight paranoia, but in the world she lived in one would have to be stupid, brainwashed, or insane not to be a little paranoid—and she was none of those things. This tendency toward anti-positive war gaming—or, to the layperson, worry-ing about things that hadn't happened yet—had its downside for sure, but she preferred the former term because there is a positive side to this particular neurosis. If controlled, it could be a major strength. When those around her were blindsided by an unforeseen circumstance, she came off looking like a genius because she had, not one but several solutions already in the works. To Lisa, there was no such thing as an unforeseen circumstance. This natural pathology wreaked havoc on her health and emotional well-being for a good part of her life until an old friend helped her to not only get it under control but to redeem it and shape it into the powerful tool that it had become. The ability to turn worry into war gaming was the character trait that was most responsible for getting her where she was today, and where she was today was in the hot seat at a world cabinet meeting about to have to address the most powerful man who ever lived.

They were well into the Babel Resurgence Project briefings by now as the line in her mind between worrying and war gaming continued to fade at an alarming rate. The administrators of each of the four sections had finished and the engineer in charge of the Physical Unification Team finished early since the major work of his team was completed. They had moved on without the expected break to the computer network administrator, and Lisa was crossing her fingers that he would be allowed to use the time yielded to him by his colleague since the Project itself was mostly on his plate at this stage. That was the only hope she could cling to at this point because crew recruitment was the next item on the agenda and she couldn't imagine that the Ruler would be pleased, to say the least, to be getting a briefing from anyone other than Dr. Abus on this subject.

Lisa removed and replaced her glasses several times and even tried to distract herself from looking toward the door by thinking about how silly it was that she wore glasses. *No one wears glasses anymore,* she thought. Eye correction procedures were as common as haircuts to those who were not simply being housed and fed like cattle for their genetic material. She started wearing them as UV protection when she first moved to the capital because she was not used to the desert sun. She immediately found that they made her feel empowered, as if she had this alter-ego that had always been screaming to get out. She was so attached to them and how they made her feel and look that she switched to transitions so she could wear them all the time, even though they had no corrective effect at all. The distraction being short lived, she continued trying not to look over her shoulder toward the door, but the more she determined not to, the more it became an involuntary response to every noise or movement behind her. After several instances of false hope caused by random cabinet staffers coming and going through the door behind her, the very dignified Dr. Abus entered and made his way to the table by way of his very intentional yet undignified gait. Lisa rose to meet him outside of the range of the table mic with the intention of briefing him as usual, but this close call made it look as if she was running to meet her father at the airport gangway after a long absence. The only thing the pseudo-emotional scene was missing was a long embrace and a kiss on the cheek. She briefed him on the meeting so far and made sure that he had received the briefing packet that she sent with the staffer who met him at the landing pad. There were so many other questions she had about his latest trip, but now was not the time and, for many of those questions, there would never be a time, so she stepped aside and made way for him to take the chair.

Dr. Abus sat down at the table in a very diplomatic fashion trying to make it appear as if it were his intention all along to only take the chair when the agenda fell to him while at the same time being very careful not to offend the Ruler with a presumptuous attitude or interrupt the proceedings. It was not five minutes later that the agenda fell to him.

He was announced by the chair, but before he could begin, a chilling voice came from the throne.

"Dr. Abus. So good of you to join us."

Sargon had a charming way about him that was very difficult to see through. Abus wasn't sure if he was being humorous, sincere, or threatening. He never knew the Ruler to be humorous before, but then again, a man of his power is not often heard with such expectations, so often times a quip or an ironic musing that would have elicited good laughs coming from someone else may fall to the floor in nervous silence coming from him. To those in the Administration he was not seen as sincere either, in the sense of genuinely caring about you as an individual. Of course, to the outside world his public persona came off as being very sincere but not to the people in this room. So, in the doctor's mind this left only threatening as the most likely intended tone. The fact that he said it in a way that made Abus feel as if he knew where he had been and what he was doing just added to the tension.

Sargon did, in fact, know where the doctor had been and what he was up to. Not just him but all of the ministers—but that was never revealed to them in any concrete way. The more they thought that they had some semblance of privacy, the more they would conduct business in a manner in which they were not intentionally trying to hide things and that made it easier for him to spy on them. He was actually quite interested in meeting this Dr. McAdams that had spawned so much intrigue in the Abus camp, but he would allow the façade to continue until Abus was ready to present him as a candidate.

"Many apologies, Your Majesty. I was on an important mission that has only recently been necessitated by the incident on Mars . . . I was only able to return to the capital within the hour, Your Majesty. I came directly here from the landing pad and I apologize if my arrival was disturbing to the proceedings in any way. I would never dishonor His Majesty by not respecting his time . . . I am most honored and unworthy to be in your presence, Majesty." This mix of nervous, explanatory pleading and phrases of protocol apparently was enough to earn him grace enough to continue.

"Relax, Abus . . ." the Ruler said in the way a coach or a drill sergeant would to embarrass an often misbehaving yet favorite underling. ". . . your briefing."

In this rare and unexpected moment of familiarity, the other ministers and staff members found themselves having to hold back smiles but quickly returned to the usual austere protocol when the briefing turned to discussion of the incident on Mars. Dr. Abus read briefly from the Space Administration's findings report and explained how the incident had affected the progress of successful crew recruitment. It wasn't simply the newly heightened fear of the realities and dangers of living in space—this was making candidates scarce for sure—but the reality was that many of the already committed department heads were on Mars at the time of the incident. Even some of the second and third in line for key positions were at the colony.

The Mars colony was the one permanent human presence outside of Earth's lunar orbit or it was until just recently. The colony was primarily a mining facility providing the Babel Resurgence Project with much-needed resources. Although it was a long journey, it was agreed that it was best to get as many resources as possible for the construction and outfitting of the vessel from non-Earth sources so as not to deplete the planet of its own necessary resources. In addition to being a mining facility, the colony was also the major research and development lab for gaining the knowledge and experience necessary for colonizing space. The administrator of the facility had been selected as Director of Colonial Development for the Babel Resurgence Project and was using the colony as a sort of boot camp for the first-generation space pioneers that would be the first to leave behind the safety of *Epoch Utopia* for a permanent, alien home. Most of the preparation for colonization was being done at the facility on Mars so, therefore, most of the key personnel were lost in the disaster.

The disaster or incident, as it was to be referred to officially, left Dr. Abus in a real bind professionally and completely undone personally. He had gotten to know all of the department heads quite well through the selection process, some of them were even old friends of his. Not only did the incident set his schedule way behind but it caused him deep personal sorrow at the loss of so many friends. He was able to eventually regain composure by logically and even callously categorizing it in his mind as training for the day of departure. The fact was that every one of these people he was responsible for and getting to know so well was eventually going to sail off into the darkness of space never to return and he would never see them again. The thought that they would, in that instance, live long, fulfilling lives helped a little, so he tried not to think about the alternative that was made so brutally obvious by the Mars incident.

No one knew for sure exactly what happened, but the Space Administration's findings report cited the cause as extreme solar activity. Mars and Earth were in opposite orbits at the time, so there were no data from any near-Earth facilities when it happened. The colony itself was completely obliterated, so there really was no human record of the event. Even the personnel ships and resource transports that were in the area were destroyed. From that, at least they knew that it wasn't strictly a planetary phenomenon. It happened so quickly that there wasn't so much as a bit of information sent in warning, distress, or explanation. The fact that Mars is further from the sun than Earth made the findings very disturbing. If a solar storm of that destructive force could reach Mars, then the only hope for Earth was its strong magnetic field—and in cosmological context, that actually was no hope at all. An extinction-level event is a cosmological certainty. The trouble is determining if it will happen today or literally a million years from now.

The Space Administration had been receiving some very non-typical data recently, within the last few decades, regarding solar activity. Non-typical meaning, anomalies that were thought to be 10,000-year events. These data were in part what inspired the Babel Resurgence Project, not that the Ruler would allow this information to go public or even be disseminated among the leadership in his own Administration, but even the thought of a possible extinction-level event on Earth while he was still bound to it was unacceptable. He wasn't so much worried about the billions that would die—people die—it was that he had insane aspirations of not only living forever but ruling forever and he thought that the technology to do both was within his grasp or at least just around the corner of history. He was not going to let anything get in his way, not even something as virtually all-powerful as the sun.

Dr. Abus's briefing was anything but brief and finally came to a close after covering the successes they had had in recruitment despite the setbacks of the Mars incident.

"In conclusion, Your Majesty . . ." Abus sat back in his chair to assure the correct posture and eye contact called for by protocol, not needing his notes to finish. "We have some very promising candidates in process right now from some very unlikely fields that have shown the extraordinary ability to successfully translate important skill sets from one context to another. With so many of our top choices in the necessary fields for the mission so unexpectedly and tragically . . ." he paused for a moment in respect for the deceased, ". . . unavailable . . . we found ourselves in the position of having to be, shall we say, more creative in our definition of an ideal candidate. As is the nature of creativity, we discovered previously untapped potential within the broadened pool that is proving to be most beneficial to the furthering of His Majesty's goals. Our latest projections show us to be overcoming the unfortunate setbacks of recent events at a rate such that the vessel will be fully staffed for Phase III departure . . . may His Majesty live forever."

With that, the chair moved the agenda forward to the next minister and, as he began droning on about the necessity of bringing certain regions of the network's physical plant up to current standards, Abus lost himself in thought being careful not to look too cognitively absent, especially after the grand entrance that elicited such unwanted attention from the Supreme Ruler. Abus could not afford to expend anymore political capital, but he also couldn't afford to waste another moment. His mind immediately got to work on ideas of how to make what he just projected manifest itself in reality while his head nodded in false affirmation of the proceedings and his eyes lied about his focus. His one focus remained Dr. Noah McAdams.

CHAPTER FIVE

Noah awoke abruptly again. Always at the same point in the reoccurring dream that had plagued him for months. The chaos, the slithering mob, the disorientation, the eternal quest, the false hope, the massive tower, the beguiling smoke, the glimmering rocket, the intense fire, and most importantly, her comforting but elusive face. The luxurious bed and silk sheets didn't help to put that particular dream to rest, but at least the aroma of genuine Ethiopian coffee brewing helped to wake him past the point of dream linger. He regained consciousness enough to wonder if they had set the timer on the coffeemaker or if someone had come in while he was asleep. He lumbered out of bed and headed to the kitchen to answer the first question of the day.

As he passed through the living area, he clicked on the viewer to start to catch up on the news, and as soon as the picture came up he immediately regressed to dream linger. He could not believe his eyes. It was a replay of the World News Network coverage of the *Interpreter One* launch and it was as if he had fallen right back into his dream. The shot of the attending crowd morphed into a shot of the tower and the billowing smoke. The noise, the shaking, the intensity of the moment, it was all the same. Finally, the coverage ended with a top view shot of the rocket coming at the camera and then the picture being overcome by the flames as the rocket escaped the camera's view.

An eerie feeling overcame him as he spotted the time and date stamp in the corner of the image. He had to check several other date sources in the apartment to try and regain his sanity. He thought he had gotten his bearings about the correct date on the aircraft on the way here. He remembered it vividly because when he asked Barney what the date was, he was a little too pleased with himself to find out that in two years of being alone on a deserted island he didn't miss a day in his accounting. It was the exact day that he thought it was. In a world where computerized calendars rule, that was quite a feat. He dropped almost lifelessly to the couch as he tried to think this through. He knew what today's date was for sure and the date stamp on the news coverage was only a few days ago, yet he had been seeing this same set of images over and over again for months. He had dreamed this before it had happened, down to the last swirl of smoke.

He was actually kind of disappointed with himself that he was finding this so hard to believe. He has always been a man of science, since even before he was a man at all, but that was only a part of the more whole, spiritual man he was. He had become, years earlier and even now was becoming, a man of faith and he found that those two things are not mutually exclusive—on the contrary, they are complements of one another.

With that thought bolstering his faith, he regained his composure, got up, and poured himself a cup of coffee, the first sip of which inspired a moan of ecstasy that may have made the neighbors wonder whether the new tenant was alone or not. If he had neighbors? He didn't really know. All he knew was that there was an armed guard at the door, so he couldn't meet the neighbors even if he wanted to. He wasn't really an "introduce yourself to the neighbors" kind of guy anyway. He was a "I think I'll strand myself on a deserted island" kind of guy, so the curiosity about the neighbors faded quite quickly. What didn't fade quickly was her face and he was glad for that.

He couldn't help but think that the only thing missing from the images of the news coverage he just saw was her perfect, unattainable face.

Not being able to shake that disappointment, he finished his coffee and went to seek solace in the shower. Although the hot water was a nice change, the experience of a normal, modern shower was forever ruined for him. He was always going to miss his own private tropical waterfall. The view, the openness, the intense pressure of thousands of liters of water cascading down and pounding the tension out of the muscles, the relaxing high afterward. Governmentally mandated low-flow shower heads and a computerized time limit shut-off didn't offer much solace, if any at all.

While dressing, Noah began to realize that possibly last night's scotch was petitioning for a second cup of coffee and he was more than happy to oblige. He had found a bean on the island that was similar to coffee, the caffeine count was even rather high, but there was nothing like the age-old perfection of a genuine Ethiopian bean. He was so distracted by his quest for genuine coffee that he almost walked right past Barney who had come in while he was showering and was enjoying a cup himself on the couch.

"Well, just make yourself at home!" Noah said sarcastically to hide the fact that he truly was startled by the old man as he caught him out of the corner of his eye.

"I haven't seen you jump like that since the time you mistook that python for a tree branch." Barney laughed, relishing the rare occasion when the shoe was on the other foot.

"So I'm a little jumpy. Sue me. You've got half of Baghdad crawling around this place keeping an eye on me," Noah said resentfully. "I haven't seen a soul in two years . . . you'd be jumpy too."

"Would be?" Barney laughed, knowing that he didn't need to explain himself further.

"Good morning!" Noah said in a playfully grumpy mood as he retrieved his cup from the coffee table and refilled it.

"How'd you sleep?" Barney asked, genuinely interested in his friend's well-being but also looking for an opening to bring the conversation back around to their unfinished business.

"Fine, fine . . . it was no bamboo cot, but I made do." Noah often attempted humor when he was trying to avoid a subject. Barney knew him well enough to sense that something was up as Noah seemed to be lost in thought.

"You okay, really?" Barney asked.

"Yeah, I'm fine . . . under the circumstances." There was a pause while each man tried to find the high ground in defining those circumstances.

Noah had illegally squatted on government property and Barney had basically blackmailed an old friend who had once saved his life. Neither one was feeling very high about their ground, but Barney attempted to spin things positively for both their sakes.

"Hey, I'm sorry it had to be like this, but if you will just hear me out I think . . . well . . . there's just a lot of things you don't know . . . you're just going to have to trust me . . ." Barney couldn't get anymore out before Noah jumped in.

"Trust you? Really? How can I trust you when I'm being held like some kind of prisoner?" Noah was growing more serious now in his tone.

"I can assure you, the prison cells here are nothing like this, my friend," Barney said, keeping his composure and allowing Noah to vent.

"I tried to make some calls last night and I was mysteriously unable. The computer said I couldn't place a communication without a personal identifier? Would you care to explain that?" Noah often had trouble governing his passion for individual liberty and personal privacy.

"Yes, sorry about that. You know I couldn't let anyone else know you're here until we get our story straight."

"Story straight? What story?" Noah said, indignant about the assumption that he had to somehow explain himself.

"Don't act naïve, Noah. I know you're well aware of the world we live in." Barney didn't need to say anymore than that to cause Noah to revert to his calculated, unemotional survival mode.

"I thought I had left that world behind," Noah said coldly then changed his expression to one of skeptical attentiveness. "Okay, how do you propose we reconcile our little situation with the world we live in?"

"Don't worry. I'm handling it," Barney said in a clandestine tone that Noah had never heard from him before but that was quite natural to the palace appointee. "Let's just say that the filename on your research permit, and grant money I might add, had been corrupted and it took my office some time to locate you. Needless to say, the Palace is not big on this whole 'off the grid' nonsense you insist on pursuing."

Noah thought for a second and then wisely said, "That's in your court. I don't intend to even address the question if posed to me, as long as I can speak plainly about where I've been for the last two years. Permits and permissions and what have you, those things don't matter to me." The last thing Noah wanted was to live a lie.

"You're acting as if a little lie to smooth things over is worse than breaking the law in the first place," Barney said with some confusion. "Let me see if I can swing a retroactive permit. It will take some doing, but I think I can do it without raising too many eyebrows."

"Thanks. That would be best, I think. That should keep those vultures over at the Parks Department off my back," Noah said with some disdain and then became lost in thought once again.

In Noah's mind, he had every right to be on that island, law or no law. He was as much a natural part of that nature preserve as anything else there. He came to that island with nothing, without even the clothes on his back. He was birthed anew out of the ocean onto that beach and simply fulfilled the potential within himself using the natural resources around him.

Noah was often astonished and usually perturbed by the hypocrisy of evolutionary naturalists who champion natural selection as the most powerful creative force in the universe and claim that man has no purpose because he is merely a product of it, reducing man to the same level as all other animals while at the same time treating mankind as if it is some sort of rapist of the natural world. He hated intellectual dishonesty, either man is simply fulfilling his natural path as a part of an evolutionary ecosystem and everything he does is natural and right according to that system of morality, or he is not. You cannot have it both ways.

This was the self-defeating philosophy of many of those administrating the preserve, but Noah, of course, did not hold to that system of morality. He had become a man of faith who was convinced that there is such a thing as purpose. That was not always so, but years ago his eyes had been opened to a greater world of thought, a much more spiritual world that, contrary to popular belief, did not oppose the scientist in him—quite the contrary, it opened new doors for the scientist in him to walk through and explore.

Noah was all for preserving and conserving life and natural resources but for the betterment of mankind, not at its expense. Too many so-called conservationists he had come across in his journeys through nature and the academic world would kill a hundred people to save one snail. Their self-defeating philosophy perplexed him so. Noah's worldview—that included faith and purpose—was the only one he had found, after years of testing and searching, that actually had standing when it came to moral high ground on the subject of conservation. He believed that the Earth was our responsibility and that we are to care for it and subdue it for the betterment of mankind. If evolutionary naturalism is followed to its natural conclusion, there is no room for concepts like responsibility and intentional betterment; there just is what there is with no purpose, yet the naturalists act as if they have the high moral ground. Noah smiled as he remembered how they seldom appreciate someone pointing this out to them and he almost laughed out loud as he recalled the title that had been bestowed upon them by the majority in the biological science community who had moved on from Darwinian evolution to the more enlightened intelligent design model. They called them the "Old Priesthood of Science." This was coming from the science community itself not from the religious community; in fact, it was meant to be a slam on both the Darwinians and the religious—attempting to lump them all in the same boat as out-of-date and uninformed. Noah thought that attempt to be less humorous seeing as the only difference between the secular ID community and those who interpreted the evidence as he did was the identity of the intelligent designer.

The Darwinian naturalists tended to congregate in the Parks Department naturally because for decades they had been worshiping the earth at the altar of manmade global climate change, the only acceptable sacrifice upon which is the death of technology and the reverting of as much of the planet to its savage state as possible with missionary zeal. They had been usurping more and more of the surface of the planet into the borders of their parks and preserves for decades until individualists like Noah had nowhere else to go but on so-called protected land. The Supreme Ruler made great use of the movement as he was taking power because it was a readymade conduit for redistributing the wealth of the planet according to his liking. Sargon allowed them to continue the practice of land usurpation after he came to power because it gave him direct administrative control over the natural resources in those parks and preserves without having to deal with the bureaucracy of the economic unions. He used many of these resources to build the earthbound facilities that provided support to the Babel

Resurgence Project. Some of the materials made it into space, but most of it was used to build the things that would be left behind. He kept the acquisition and use of the resources very quiet. The naturalists at the Parks Department turned a blind eye after a few of their colleagues, who had been a little too vocal about their discontent with the situation, disappeared mysteriously. This was one reason why Dr. Abus thought he wouldn't have a problem pushing through a retroactive permit for Noah without too many questions asked. Lately there had been a lot of "no questions asked" paperwork going through that department. Surely something coming from the desk of a Palace Appointee would be treated thusly.

In a similar way that the Darwinian naturalists migrated to the Parks Department, the intelligent design crowd, the secular version that is, migrated to the space program. The Babel Resurgence Project was teeming with them. They had succumbed to the reality that irreducible complexity in biological systems and the presence of encoded digital information in DNA, along with a great many other things, could not be statistically accounted for through randomness. The very definition of random is the absence of design.

For over a hundred years they used the language of design and purpose to describe and discuss biology while being very careful to include the disclaimer that what they really meant is "the appearance of design," because there was simply no other way to have an intelligent conversation about such things without such a vocabulary. As time went on and technology enabled science to peer deeper and deeper into the universe of the microscopic, they discovered some very startling things about life as we know it, not the least of which was that when they were calling us biological machines, with tongue firmly implanted in cheek, they were more accurate than they had imagined.

Inside the cell, they found biological machines manufacturing proteins from a blueprint that was digitally encoded by those very proteins. Regardless of the fact that information doesn't come about without an intelligent source, it is an entirely new problem to solve when the information needed to manufacture a thing is itself the thing being manufactured. The paradox of the chicken and the egg had met its match and there was no purposeless answer of randomness to be found. What had been talked about as the appearance of design was now openly talked about as actual design. This didn't happen overnight of course. It took generations for the old school—those who had lifetimes of work at stake—to die off and relinquish the power of peer review and grant money.

It was as much an issue of personal morality as it was one of science and that caused much willful blindness. The moral issue was simply this: if there is truly design, then there is truly a designer, the existence of which necessitates a morality outside of oneself. The new reality of the biological sciences quickly split into several camps: one agnostic about the identity of the designer, thus ignoring the whole moral question altogether; one restoring the enlightenment science of Newton and others who founded modern science on the assumption of a supreme being as creator; and finally those who gravitated to the space program and specifically the Babel Resurgence Project, who were expecting to sail off into space and find their designer in the form of little green men. This became a very popular view as mankind came to grips with the reality of interplanetary space travel—after all, if we were traveling to other planets, who's to say that some other race somewhere else in the universe couldn't have traveled here. This also was an attempt, albeit unconscious, to do away with the morality question because what they were really attempting to do was create their creator in their own image, once again putting themselves at the center of the moral universe.

It was this latter group that Noah considered to be particularly short-sighted. After all, the only thing they were doing was delaying an infinite regression by one generation.

When considering infinity, a movement of one unit on any scale is meaningless. The question still remained: who made the little green men? Their shortsightedness was due to their unwillingness to admit that one can spiral down the wormhole of causation only so long before having to make a leap of faith. In the positive, there is the leap to a self-existent "uncaused cause"; and in the negative, there is the leap to nothingness. Either way, a leap of faith is unavoidable. This fact puts the morality question at the very center of the matter. It defines the whole scientific quest of origins as a spiritual quest at its very core, and this is what causes willful blindness among so many in the scientific community.

The world had become quite hedonistic as a result of this willful blindness. If the natural is all there is, then satisfying natural drives and pursuing tactile sensation becomes the highest calling. It follows that gluttonous tendencies toward food, drink, drugs, and sexual expression are only vices if one is not the center of one's own moral universe, and treating others with respect and worth is much easier if that respect and worth has only oneself as the measure. It is much easier to choose a philosophy of science that does not interfere with one's philosophy of life than it is to look the consequences of that philosophy in the face and attempt the needed reconciliation between self and others or admit the self-destructiveness of such behavior.

With such self-destructiveness at the center of this worldview, it should have been no surprise to Noah that many could accept into their philosophy so many self-defeating arguments such as: there is no such thing as truth, or it's possible to get information from randomness, or God doesn't exist. All one need do is define the terms within the arguments and it becomes quite apparent that they do not stand. If there is no truth, then the statement that there is no truth is not true. The simple act of denying truth reveals its existence. The very definition of truth necessitates its existence; the very definition of randomness is the absence of the existence of information; and the very definition of God—the Supreme Being, beyond which nothing greater can even be imagined—includes existence, for certainly a real such being is greater than an imaginary one. He has, after all, been revealing Himself as just that self-existent uncaused cause since before human history. It is the very name He gave us by which to refer to Him.

Noah was not surprised by the leap from self-destruction to self-defeating arguments; he was simply perplexed by the intellectual dishonesty. Although, as he remembered his own faults, temptations, and broken relationships, it was easier to see the reason for it. For those who are not aware of the grace extended by that One toward those with faults, temptations, and broken relationships, it all becomes impossible to bear and they are relegated to placating themselves with attempted self-gratification and vain philosophies, however illogical.

Noah realized he was lost in thought and that Barney was staring silently in an attempt to get him to say what's on his mind. It was an old negotiation tool that had helped him ascend to his prestigious position. Until now Barney had reverted to interacting with Noah as the old friend that knew all his quirks, but at this point he was clearly Dr. Abus, Palace Appointee. Noah gave in and tried to diplomatically summarize all that had been going through his mind.

"Barney, I think you know that I don't exactly share the same worldview as the rest of the people you've recruited for this project."

"Exactly, that's why you're here," Dr. Abus said in brief counterpoint before returning to the silent stare.

"No, I don't think you understand. I don't just mean that, you know . . . I'm a rugged individualist with little patience for socially engineered tyranny and all that. It's deeper than that . . . more . . . more serious than that, I'm afraid." Noah lifted his gaze from the spot on the floor where he'd been staring to meet Dr. Abus's eyes.

"It's a woman, isn't it!" Barney blurted, briefly reverting to old friend status.

"No, no . . . that's not what I'm trying to say!" Noah said, caught off guard by words that fell closer to home than Barney knew. They both locked back into the power stare and Noah continued. "I don't believe in the Project. I see it as foolish and well, frankly, suicidal. There's just no room in my worldview for the possibility of its success. I am not the guy you're looking for. I thought you knew that about me?"

Dr. Abus tried to respond but was also caught off guard by words that hit too close to home. He had been surrounded for so long by Sargon's yes men that he had actually never heard anyone say that out loud. Though Barney suspected there were others who felt the same way about it as he did, himself, he never expected to hear the words actually spoken. It was actually refreshing to him and served to convince him even more that he had the right man.

"That is exactly the type I'm looking for at this point, Noah. Someone has to insert some sanity into this thing. It's that attitude that could end up saving countless lives put in jeopardy by the overzealous and arrogant narcissists running this thing."

Noah stopped trying to explain since he didn't think Barney was keying in on the spiritual nature of his objections. He simply didn't see room in his biblically based worldview for mankind permanently escaping the confines of the Earth. He had read to the end of the book and it just wasn't an option as far as he was concerned. The fact that they were actually about to do it was unsettling and exciting to him all at the same time. It meant that either the end was very near or that there was about to be a catastrophe so dire that the end would be wished for. He was sure that Barney was aware of the spiritual context of his life and life's work—they had many conversations about it. Although it was a long time ago that they had become friends, even before his spiritual rebirth, he hoped that he had changed enough for the better over the years of their friendship that Barney would see the reality of it.

"Did it occur to you that if I said yes, I would be one of those lives being put in jeopardy?" Noah replied, changing the tack of his argument.

Barney's face went white as he tried not to think about all of those lost in the Mars incident. "Noah, when I said that there are things you don't know . . . well . . . to answer your question, yes. There is not a minute that goes by that it doesn't occur to me. I fight every day to keep it out of the front of my mind . . ." His eyes welled up slightly as his words trailed off.

"What is it, Barnard?" Noah asked. He had never seen his friend like this before and was quite concerned.

"There has already been an accident . . . an incident . . . well, we don't even know what really happened."

"What happened?" Noah asked again, softly.

"The colony on Mars was destroyed by some kind of anomalous solar activity." Abus could see the next question coming, so he saved his friend from having to ask. "There were no survivors. Even the ships in the area were destroyed." There was a short silence then Dr. Abus concluded the subject as if he were back at the cabinet briefing. "It was a training ground for the Project and most of the department heads were there when it happened, not to mention a good portion of the crew. I knew many of them personally, I put them there. Believe me when I say it has occurred to me. I'm not blowing smoke when I say that I need someone of your . . . sanity . . . your faith . . . along. After everything that's happened, I need someone I can trust to help fill the void."

"What exactly would I be saying yes to, I mean, what exactly are you asking me to do?" Noah asked, surprised at how close his own question was to a yes.

"I need a Director of Colonial Development and I'm convinced you're the man for the job. You're the most brilliant and resourceful man I've ever met, and if I'm forced to send people into the wilderness of space and leave them stranded and alone amongst the stars along the way, there is no one I could possibly trust more with their safety, no one who could possibly increase their chances of survival more than you could. You more than exceed the educational requirements for the position and you stand head and shoulders above anyone in the scientific community as far as discoveries turned into useful technologies—you practically singlehandedly cured cancer and you're not even an M.D. All this before you were twenty! Until just recently you were the chair of a very prestigious engineering department and your theories on particle physics are part of what is making this whole project possible. I just went to pick you up on an island where you literally arrived naked and alone two years earlier only to find you living like a king with electricity and refrigeration. You practically flaunted your genius in my face; you gave me a mixed drink with ice in it. I almost expected you to pull out a computer made out of bamboo and rat intestines."

"That was my next project," Noah said in an attempt to break up this uncomfortable recitation of his heroic accomplishments. They both laughed and it served to release some of the tension in the room.

"Noah, you are an explorer at heart. You're more at home discovering new things than . . . well, I can't even think of anywhere else you'd feel at home. It's your nature to not only ask how but to ask why and for that matter, why not. Most importantly, you care about people. I know you're a little out of practice at that, but you're a natural leader and that will come back to you. What else can I say besides you're fearless, practically suicidal . . ." Abus paused as if officiating a moment of silence. ". . . but, as we have already discussed, that is, unfortunately, what this challenge requires. I know you don't see it in the cards or whatever you religious types say, but you *are* the man for the job."

Noah was speechless. Though he was uncomfortable listening to such praise lauded upon him, he was more convinced than he expected he would be when the conversation began. Dr. Abus made a good argument. It was just that Noah could not make a decision like this without getting some wise council.

"I'm not saying yes, but . . ." Noah searched for the reason for the "but" while Barney waited with baited breath.

". . . but?" Barney said to try to close the sale.

"Just let me make some calls," Noah said reluctantly.

"It is a woman, isn't it!" Barney teased. "I'm having fun, but in all seriousness, that is part of the equation that must be considered. If there *is* someone special, well . . . well let's just say that you need to take care of that sooner rather than later. If you don't make that choice, it will be made for you. Just being up front with you about the conditions of crew membership."

"Way to close the sale," Noah said sarcastically.

"No, really, is there someone special?" Barney said back in friend mode.

"I can only hope." Noah sighed. "I didn't exactly leave a forwarding address when I left."

"What's her name?"

"Ruth," Noah whispered.

"Here . . ." Abus handed him the earpiece that had been set up for him by security. "Call whomever you would like, just give me a few hours to get this in process."

"Thanks." Noah reluctantly took the instrument of the death of his liberty and privacy and stood up with Barney to see him out. "I'm going to need to head back to North America while I'm getting this all sorted out."

"Of course. Here is the account number to your *grant money*." Barney winked.

"Ah . . ." Noah started to protest.

Abus stopped him. "Just think of it as a sign-on bonus. How else are you going to get there? I suppose you could build a plane out of the couch and the microwave, but this would be quicker." They both laughed one last time. "You can leave this afternoon. Read this on the way." He handed him a small e-pad. "It's the Space Administration's Findings Report. I'm sure you have many questions. There are also a series of briefings about the Project to get you started . . . on your decision I mean . . . I'm not assuming . . ."

"Thanks . . . I'll see you soon," Noah said without an ounce of deception as he closed the door behind Barney.

Dr. Abus trusted his old friend and didn't detect any intrigue in him, but all the same he left instructions with the security detail to tail him covertly.

Alone again, Noah slumped on the couch in front of the viewer and reluctantly put his new earpiece in. He sat for an hour trying to get the courage up then finally said, "Ruth Evans."

"Searching . . ." the computer said, and then just before it was about to ask him for more specific information, he recanted.

"Cancel!" There was a short silence and then a new command. "Nearest airport, please."

CHAPTER SIX

It was coming closer . . . closer . . . he couldn't get away. There was nowhere to go . . . emptiness all around. The face . . . the face in the sun . . . the face consuming the sun. It was brighter than the sun. *He* was brighter than the sun. Larger . . . larger . . . all encompassing, all consuming yet never consumed. Intense heat, a fiery sword . . . lashing out from the face in the sun, from the One consuming the sun. The One . . . The One . . . The One . . . no hiding, no escaping, no running. All is revealed, all is exposed . . . every dark corner of the mind brought to light . . . every thought, every deed . . . no escape!

"TURN!"

The thundering voice in the dream woke him once again. Afzal Jamail Sargon ruled everywhere but in his dreams. As always, he switched on the light, wiped the sweat from his face, and sat up on the edge of the magnificently opulent bed to wait for the passing of dream linger. It disturbed him so every time it happened, but he knew that before long he would return to the physical completely and forget it ever happened. Even after so many times, like any dream, this one would dive back into the subconscious only to resurface at the behest of a random trigger. A bright light in his eyes, a raging fire, or perhaps a clap of thunder—these things would all eventually bring it screaming back to the front of his mind, but until then it would be as if it had never happened.

His favorite wife awoke to see him, once again, disturbed and hunched over the edge of the bed. This time there were still several hours before his day was to begin, so she hesitantly placed her hands on his shoulders in an attempt to release the tension. Every word spoken to the Ruler was a gamble, so she remained quiet. To touch the Ruler unsolicited was dangerous even for her—she had her bruises to remind her of that. Many times she wasn't even allowed to sleep in his chamber and she was the favorite. It was more dangerous, however, for him not to be consoled. Not that he personally had a need to be coddled, but it was less dangerous for those around him if he wasn't in the type of mood that his disturbed sleep put him in, so those closest to him, for their own sakes, did everything within their power to ensure a good night's sleep for him.

He accepted the gesture and toppled face down into his pillow. She turned out the light and continued rubbing his shoulders in the darkness. Eventually he drifted off to some last remaining dark shadow in his dreams where he would cower and shake for the rest of the night in an attempt to stay out of the light. She knew she would not sleep. There was always an eerie coldness in the room after the initial dream was gone. He always slept through it as if he longed for it, but she was always disturbed for the rest of the night. She laid back, closed her eyes, and tried to think of sunrise, but there was no getting around the fact that this was going to be a long night.

* * *

Noah opened his eyes only to shield them with his right arm as he reached for the shade handle with the other. He had the feeling that he was dreaming but he couldn't remember about what. It's possible that the changing air pressure, the subtle low frequency hum of the engines, and the slight rocking back and forth only gave him the illusion of dreaming. What was the difference? He has felt as if he has been in a constant dream ever since he dozed off in his hammock on the beach. The déjà vu he was experiencing at the moment from the sun in his eyes and the aircraft noises only added to the confusion. He was already confused enough about what to tell Barney and, more importantly, how to confront Ruth after all this time. Noah slammed the sliding shade on the aircraft window shut in a very poor attempt to relieve his frustration. Those around him jumped slightly or turned toward him instinctively with the kind of looks that served to remind him that he was back in society again and he could no longer do as he pleased and he certainly could not act out irrationally. He apologized quietly and put his nose back in the briefing pad that Dr. Abus gave him, hoping that they would all retract back into their own little worlds as before and leave him to his.

He was still getting used to people again and the crowds at the airport and the confined environment of the commercial aircraft were particularly challenging for him, more challenging than he had imagined. He was about to ask for another drink to help take his mind off the many challenges he was facing, but before he could get the attendant's attention, the landing preparation announcement convinced him otherwise. The announcement itself helped more than the drink would have as it renewed his excitement about where he was headed and who he was about to see. If there was anything on Earth that could possibly give him the feeling of returning home it would be sitting around the dinner table with Martha and Peter, and if anyone could help him through this confusion it was Peter.

Peter and Martha Abrams were the closest thing to parents Noah had known since his own parents passed when he was about twelve. They were more than surrogate parents though; they were good friends and, more importantly, spiritual mentors. It was Peter who was largely responsible for the spiritual awakening that began in Noah those many years ago. Noah could still remember the first time they met and how from the very first word that came out of his mouth Noah could not help but feel as if wisdom was his native tongue. He wasn't an overly educated man or a child prodigy like Noah. His was an ancient wisdom that came with a love for people and a peaceful disposition that transcended circumstances. He introduced Noah to a life-changing eternal perspective that made his once crippling pain and inner struggle fade away into insignificance. It wasn't acumen that won him over, just a simple, quiet invitation to admit bias, face truth, and decide what to do with it. No grandiloquent arguments or attempts to masquerade blind faith as real faith, just a peaceful smile and a gentle nudge toward the truth—the truth of a faith that stands rock solid on evidence, a faith placed in the only object worthy of true faith.

Peter seemed so old to him back then, twenty years ago. Noah wasn't sure if it was because of the ancient wisdom or simply because of the fact that Noah himself was not even twenty when they met. He was hoping to find that the last few years had been gracious to his old friends and he sent a quick prayer out as he remembered that Martha was not in very good health the last time he had seen them. The moving sidewalk seemed to be too slow for his anxious feet as he was thinking about seeing his old friends, so he started walking briskly past those who were content with the speed and direction of the path laid out for them. He had disembarked the aircraft in plenty of time to catch the Mag-Lev out to the station near their place, but he was so excited, in his own subdued way, that he couldn't just stand there when it was within his power to go faster and farther toward the goal.

The ride on the Mag-Lev was uneventful, so it gave Noah a chance to continue reading the material Dr. Abus had given him. The Findings Report was quite unsettling, and as he put it down he had a deep feeling of regret in the pit of his stomach stemming from his attempt to make Barney feel bad about asking him to endanger himself. He felt like a first-class heel. He had never seen Barney so moved, yet at the same time he was so determined to make sure that their sacrifice was not for nothing. That actually was Noah's mission in life, to make sure that people know that it is not for nothing—life, that is—and that the leap of faith that is inevitable does not have to be to nothing. Even now it seemed as if Noah was convincing himself that there may be some higher calling in this whole madness after all. If anyone could help him separate madness from providence and sort this all out, it was Peter.

Even the high-speed train didn't seem fast enough to keep up with his thoughts as they screamed from the Abramses to Barney to the Babel Resurgence Project. Although they never really landed, no matter where Noah's thoughts were, they were orbiting around Ruth. He couldn't quite bring himself to think about her in his normal dispassionate, analytical manner, so until he could confide in Peter and Martha that she was foremost on his mind, he admired thoughts of her from afar.

He was hoping the walk from the station to their place would settle his thoughts a little and as the door slid open, the blast of fresh air started to do just that. It wasn't the oxygen-induced breeze coming from the direction of a tropical waterfall surrounded by virgin rainforest, but compared to the stale air of the pressurized Mag-Lev car it was refreshing. He was going to have to learn to stop comparing everything to his time on the island, but in the meantime at least it brought him back there in his mind, albeit fleetingly.

The walk did calm him some, but he found himself walking faster and faster as he neared their door. It was very out of character for Noah to be so anxious, but as he rang the bell and the door cracked open, his anxiety melted away and he rediscovered the man he once was. The door swung wide after the initial tentative peek and there was nothing but silence as a white-haired man with a goatee stood dumbfounded. His eyes immediately welled up and before tears could be witnessed escaping, he reached out and embraced Noah with arms too powerful for a man of his age. Peter looked a little older than Noah was hoping, but he still had his strength and his passion for life and people. Noah could tell that before he even uttered a word.

Peter finally got his wits about him and let out a boisterous laugh before he managed to loosen his death grip only to grab him by the shoulders to hold him at arm's length so he could get a good look at him.

"Noah! What are you doing here?" Peter exclaimed. "Ya know, ya coulda let us know you were back in town . . . in town? Ya coulda let us know you were still alive!"

"Well, you know me, not much for net communication, besides, I always love seeing your face after you fear I have fallen off the face of the Earth." Noah tried not to let the irony of his last statement ruin the moment. They would be discussing his possible absence from the face of the Earth soon enough.

"Come in, come in . . . Martha!" he yelled jubilantly to his wife as he ushered Noah in the door and through the hall. He was more pushing Noah to where Martha was than he was calling Martha to them since she was having trouble getting around. They burst into the living area where Martha was reclining and before she could look up from her crocheting, Peter practically yelled, "Look who's here!"

"Noah!" she nearly screamed herself as she tried to get up to embrace him.

"No, no . . . don't get up." Noah got down on one knee next to her chair as if he were asking her forgiveness for his absence and his failure to call. He allowed her to hug him around the neck for as long as she wanted and he gently rubbed her back as she wept softly into his shoulder. It was as if he was holding the shell of the woman she once was. He was careful to be gentle, though it was hard; he wanted to squeeze her as he always had, but he knew that her condition would not allow that. The doctors were still unable to put a name to it, but they were sure that she had contracted it while in the jungle where they had first met. She had some sort of neurological disorder that caused pain, randomly around her body and kept her in an almost constant state of nausea. There were no tumors or lesions on the brain, just random pain. It was baffling to everyone that knew, but most people who came into contact with her had no idea; she had such a wonderful disposition, the pain rarely showed through. Eventually, though, she became frail and partially immobile.

After a few moments of soaking in the motherly embrace and the familiar smell of something wonderful baking, he opened his eyes and was immediately thrust back into the confusion he had come there to abate. Martha had the World News Network up on the viewer with the sound muted as she was crocheting. They had a very old view screen that was only 2D, but Noah was startled to see what looked like a 3D image in it. He wasn't startled that it was 3D; in fact, he didn't even know that the viewer didn't even have that capability, he was startled at the image itself. WNN was again replaying the launch of the *Interpreter One*, the very same footage that he saw after waking from last night's dream, but this time there was a disconcerting addition. Because it was so old, the viewer didn't have a glare-free surface and it was reflecting the image being projected by the digital picture frame on the shelf behind Martha's chair. There were probably hundreds of images cycling through the slideshow, but at the moment Noah opened his eyes and the movement of the images caught his attention, there just happened to be a series of images featuring Ruth predominantly. The glare on the viewer was almost mirror-like at the low angle he was viewing it from and it made Ruth's image from the digital frame look as if it were intentionally ghosted over the top of the news footage. Noah gasped audibly as he witnessed the very same images of Ruth appear suddenly and then disappear mockingly overtop of the exact images of the crowd, the tower, the rocket, the smoke, and the blinding light that he had been dreaming night after night for months.

Martha and Peter couldn't see the reflected images from where they were—in fact, the only place in the entire universe that one could witness exactly what Noah had been dreaming all this time was that humble spot on the floor next to Martha and only from the prostrated position that he had assumed. His face must have gone white because as he brought his head up to where they could see his face again they both immediately went from expressions of joyful tearfulness to genuine concern.

"Noah, are you all right?" Martha gasped as Peter instinctively helped him to his feet and over to the couch.

Noah felt inadequate as he realized he was being helped to the couch by an eighty-year-old man and even more so as he realized he didn't have the words to tell them what was wrong. "I'm okay . . . it's . . . it's nothing . . . just give me a . . . I'll be okay."

Peter flashed into the kitchen to retrieve a glass of water and stood over him like a protective silverback as Noah drank the whole thing down, all while Martha soothed him by taking his hand and patting it as if she was trying to wake him from a bad dream.

"Just sit there for a moment. You must have had an eventful trip. You'll be fine if you just rest a while," Martha said in a faithful tone.

Noah *was* tired. He was suffering from the type of jet lag that only comes from attempting to function normally in the three furthest points from each other on the face of the planet that one can possibly be within a forty-eight-hour period, but that wasn't what was wrong and he knew it. He knew, but how was he going to explain it to them? He didn't really want to explain it but, after all, he had come here to gain from their wisdom, and how could they give him good advice if he didn't tell them what was really going on?

"Thank you," Noah whispered as he handed the empty glass back to Peter who was standing over him like a granite statue.

"Would you like some more?" he asked before taking a step back.

"No, thank you, I'm fine now," Noah assured his concerned friends.

"I know what you need . . . a good cup of coffee," Peter said as he looked for a visceral response from Noah. He got one and dashed off to the kitchen again to brew the ancient homeopathic remedy.

"What's wrong, dear?" Martha asked after a moment of wise silence.

"I'm just a little shaken up, that's all," Noah said, trying to buy some time for Peter to return. It was going to be hard enough to verbalize everything happening inside, so he certainly didn't want to have to do it twice.

"So what have you been up to for the past couple of years?" Peter shouted from the other room as if sensing the awkward silence and trying not to sound slighted or accusatory.

"Well . . ." Noah shouted back until he saw Peter leaning on the doorpost between the two rooms. "I was . . . I was unavailable. I'm sorry I couldn't keep in touch. I was in the jungle again and you know me, I don't take my earpiece into the jungle."

This answer seemed to appease their potential despondency. They first met him in the jungle twenty years ago and knew that it was his nature to lose himself in the wilderness from time to time. They could in no way take it personally that he hadn't spoken to them in years any more than they could blame their cat for wasting a beautiful afternoon by napping on a sunlit windowsill. Cats do their prowling alone and at night. Dr. Noah McAdams has always had a sort of wild, nocturnal streak in him, but he always came out of the wilderness—actual or metaphorical—with a trophy thought to have been indomitable by one lone hunter. They knew this about him and they knew better than anyone that, although it seemed to others that he was in the wilderness alone, he was by no means alone.

"If it makes you feel any better . . . you're the first people I've come to visit since I've been back to civilization." Noah continued his appeasement with a playful smile that looked as if it came with a halo that he simply forgot to put on. "I haven't seen anyone else yet, except for Bar . . . uh . . . Dr. Abus."

"How does he rate above us?" Peter blurted in the same playful manner.

"Yeah, well . . . that wasn't my choice," Noah said resentfully. "I wasn't quite done with my little wilderness experiment, but, apparently, he thought differently and it's kind of hard to argue with an old friend who has an armed security detail."

"He sent an armed detail to go find you?" Peter asked in disbelief.

"No . . . he came to find me himself," Noah said in a serious tone that only resulted in more disbelief from his dear friends. "That's kind of why, well . . . you have clearly seen that I'm struggling with something and . . . you can probably imagine why Dr. Abus came to find me."

"I know you have a history, but he's a cabinet minister?" Peter said, still unable to reconcile the information with his understanding of reality. "What's he doing trouncing around the jungle?"

"Well, it's not like I was in the middle of the Amazon," Noah explained, "I was on a small island in the Pacific and I think someone gave me up. One day Dr. Abus landed on my beach while I was takin a nap and here I am."

"Why . . . I mean, what did he want?" Martha asked, knowing that she was not going to like the answer. She knew what Dr. Abus's job was in the Administration and she knew that the two of them knew each other. Until now it hadn't occurred to her that eventually he would be calling on Noah. It was hard enough for Peter and her to deal with Noah's long absences as it was; she really didn't know if she could handle knowing for sure that they would never see him again.

Noah thought for a second then tried to explain, as much to himself as to his friends. "He says he needs my help . . . that lives depend on it. I don't know . . . he seems to have been deeply affected personally by the Mars incident. He took it really hard. He feels responsible for putting all those people in harm's way and for some reason he thinks my involvement would somehow . . . well, to be honest I don't know what he's thinking."

"What, specifically is he asking you to do?" Peter asked, completely forgetting about the coffee and taking a seat next to Noah.

"He offered me the recently vacant Director of Colonial Development position."

"Doesn't he know how you feel about the whole thing?"

"I tried to tell him, but he said that's exactly why I'm the man for the job."

"What?" they both said in a unison that only comes with sixty years of marriage.

"He said he needed someone of my . . . sanity and faith . . . to . . . let me see, how did he put it? . . . save countless lives put in jeopardy by the overzealous and arrogant narcissists running this thing."

"He actually used the word *faith*?" Peter was astonished. "It sounds to me that there is more happening here than meets the eye."

"That's an understatement," Noah said under his breath as he returned to the haunted demeanor that spawned the conversation.

"What's wrong dear, really?" Martha asked in a motherly tone that made it hard for him not to spill everything.

Noah thought hard but couldn't bring himself to verbalize the two things that were causing his uncharacteristic melancholy. He knew they were the only two people on earth that would truly understand, but that didn't seem to help. Just saying out loud that he has been having a recurring prophetic dream was almost beyond his faith and he has never been able to speak openly of matters of the heart, at least not since he was young and innocent. This latter inability is mostly responsible for his current single status and his recent wilderness experiment or more accurately, escape.

When Noah was younger, the death of his parents devastated him emotionally. They were so suddenly ripped from him in an unexplainable accident that it left him standing alone in the emotional jet-wash. He didn't have the ability to cope, so he turned inward, never letting anyone get too close. The time came when he finally let someone in, someone who had been there the whole time and who knew what he was going through, only to be devastated again. She also was taken from him. This was long before he met Ruth and he had grown and healed in so many ways, but when Ruth started getting serious about their future together, Noah shut down once again. He didn't immediately flee to the wilderness as he always had but he might as well have. The emotional wilderness he subjected her to was a much more cruel and harsh environment. After he drove her away, it took about a year or so, but finally he could stand it no more; life with her was painful and life without her was unbearable, so he fled once again to the actual wilderness.

Martha could see his wheels turning, so she artfully acted as if she were letting it go and changing the subject. "So you haven't seen anyone else since you've been back?"

Noah knew she was referring to Ruth and had kind of missed the motherly women's intuition that had so often steered him in the right direction. This particular insight was rather uncomfortable though. It made him feel as if she could see right through him and made him wonder if she were not somewhat of a prophetess herself.

"No, no one." Noah looked up and took on a sincere demeanor. "I really needed to come and talk to the two of you first. I could really use some of your wisdom and loving straight talk right now."

"Well, sweetie, if you'll just let us know what's go'n on up there in that genius head of yours we'll be happy to lead you down the wrong path as always." Martha had a way of always knowing when to lighten the mood. They all laughed and sat back in their chairs feeling the sense of family return to the living room for the first time since Noah disappeared.

"I'll tell you what, let's have some coffee and some of Martha's famous sweet rolls and we'll figure this out together." Peter jumped up, flashed into the kitchen, and returned with a tray of coffee cups and pastry before Noah and Martha could start up a meaningful conversation.

Noah took one bite and leaned over to give Martha a kiss on the cheek. "You have no idea how much I have missed this."

"So, you have been asked to be the Director of Colonial Development on mankind's first manned space expedition to attempt to leave the solar system," Peter stated precisely and in a matter-of-fact manner as he took a sip of his coffee while looking at Noah over the top of his glasses.

Noah, having returned to a feeling of safety and acceptance that only comes from being with family also returned to his typical intellectual, problem-solving personality. He started to see Peter's statement as the problem statement of an engineering equation. This was Peter's intention because he knew that Noah had it within him to figure this out. He knew that if he and Martha provided the emotional safety net, Noah would take the leap from what he knew in his head to what he knew in his heart.

". . . and therein lies the problem," Noah added to the statement.

"Define the problem as you see it, Noah," Peter encouraged.

"Problem? *Problems*, I think," Noah began. "Let's just put aside the problem of leaving everyone and everything I've ever known, the very Earth itself—forever, mind you—not one of my temporary wilderness excursions that always had the hope of return lingering in the back of my mind driving me on . . . let's just put all that aside as purely an emotional hurdle that can be overcome. That leaves us with the intellectual and the spiritual. You know far better than I about the spiritual—or maybe a better word is *biblical*—problem, so let me just verbalize the intellectual or the scientific problem. We simply do not have the science. This mission is a death sentence to all who are foolish enough to climb aboard or best-case scenario, a death sentence to their grandchildren, but eventually the vastness of space will swallow up the arrogant. The distances are greater than even the laws of physics can overcome in the lifespan of the entirety of Adam's race. At current technology levels, we'll be lucky to get two generations away from our little terrarium called Earth without succumbing to the vast energy and resource desert of interstellar space, not to mention the infinitely insurmountable vastness of intergalactic space. Need I even go any further?"

"Well that certainly does define the confines of humanity and its almost insurmountable arrogance, but it is only almost insurmountable arrogance. We both know that personally." Peter brought the topic back around to the spiritual focus that Noah was really there to talk to him about. Noah knew the science and technology involved infinitely better than Peter did and for that matter, better than most of the scientists already involved in the Project. Noah was there to benefit from the ancient wisdom that Peter had acquired through an over sixty-year personal relationship with the Ancient of Days.

"There is just no room in my worldview for humanity escaping the confines of Earth, much less the solar system, in any permanent manner—and more importantly, I just don't see how it's right for me to be involved in such an arrogantly humanistic and atheistic endeavor." Noah got right to the point.

"Then why are you even struggling with this?" Peter cornered him.

Noah looked at him with an expression of reluctant confession as he thought in the awkward silence Peter was providing for him until he could no longer stay silent himself. "Because I think God's telling me to go."

There was another silence, but this time it was more reverent than awkward, then Peter spoke up again, "Did it ever occur to you that such an endeavor is exactly where a person of faith is needed most?" He let that sink in before adding, "Many a prophet has found himself in the middle of just such an endeavor."

"You're right." Noah nodded as he thought about the Scripture he had just read on the aircraft before immersing himself in the briefings that Barney had provided.

Before he could tell them what he was thinking, Peter continued, "What if Joseph hadn't stayed true to the One True and Living God in the midst of a system that was antagonistic to that One True God? He was put there for a purpose and he not only lived and worked within it, he was put in charge over it. What if he had refused to engage with it because it was pagan and corrupt?"

Noah sighed. "I just read that passage this morning."

"What if Daniel had refused to do his best and show himself to be competent before kings? What if instead he hid his gifts from a world system that he thought may only try to use them for evil?" Peter said with a seriousness that was not devoid of joy.

"I just read that one last night." Noah shook his head in astonishment.

"I guess what I am getting at is this: is God not higher than man's intentions? Does He not use for His purposes what men only purpose for evil? Does He not cause all things to work together for the good of those who love Him and are called according to His purpose? Has He not already written the end of the book?" Peter said confidently.

"Yes. That's why I'm confused by this whole thing. Either the end is here any moment or I have misunderstood a great many things," Noah said while squinting one eye.

"Well, this whole Project does seem to cast a fresh light onto Deuteronomy 30:4," Peter said in harmony with Noah's amazement about the hinge point of history in which they found themselves.

He could see Noah doing the rapid back-and-forth movement of his eyes that he did when trying to access something in his computer-like memory, so Peter saved him the arduous task and quoted the verse, as closely to an original word-for-word translation as possible. And as he often did, Peter spoke in the Hebrew syntax that would seem awkward to non-language scholars but came naturally to the two of them: "If of your be any driven out to the uttermost parts of heaven, from there will gather YHWH your God you and from there will he fetch."

Now Peter could see the scowl on Martha's face that always came before she scolded him for talking over people's heads, so he rephrased in the more modern language of the English Standard Version: "If your outcasts are in the uttermost parts of heaven, from there the LORD your God will gather you, and from there he will take you."

There was a short silence as the implications of the verse set in, then Peter continued.

"There's one thing I've learned in my many years on this Earth and that's this: my years are not really many." Peter saw the confusion on Noah's face so he continued, "What I mean is, we have a finite nature that projects itself onto the infinite. We automatically define things as having a beginning and an end, so when God says to us 'In the beginning . . .' He is basically saying '. . . and this is where you come in, you don't need to know what came before that right now.' And when He says 'the end is near,' it's only the end in an anthropomorphic sense. In a way that satisfies our finite bent."

"Yeah, I understand that. I'm just trying to reconcile what I know from Scripture with what I'm seeing now. Normally that wouldn't be such a big deal for me, you know—I live by faith, but this time it's very personal and overwhelming," Noah said humbly.

"Let me put it like this . . . Every generation since God started speaking about the future has tried to read into that prophecy the things they saw happening around them. But when it comes to the end, none of them have been right yet, ultimately." They both smiled at the obvious nature of the statement, a nature that is all too often overlooked. Peter continued, "What you have to remember is history, true history—not that drivel they teach in the government schools—is cyclical. It's a grand epic of a war in the heavenlies spiraling toward eternity . . . the proverbial battle between good and evil, except that it's not merely proverbial, it *is* the greater reality. The spiritual realm is more real than where you and I abide now. We tend to think of it as less real somehow and many, sadly, even consider it purely imaginary. We're merely in the shadow of the greater spiritual reality, like the two-dimensional darkness being cast on the ground by a three-dimensional bird soaring high above. For one to define or describe that majestic creature only after experiencing its shadow would be quite inadequate and frankly, tragic, yet that's exactly what many do while trying to describe their own existence. If you can learn to look at history through spiritual eyes. it will help you to look at your present—yes, and even your future—through spiritual eyes. History is a series of spiritual battles in which evil rises and attempts to bring about its arrogant tyranny on its own timetable before being thwarted, for a time, until the appointed ultimate demise it will face according to God's timetable. This has happened over and over again since before Adam's race arrived on the scene. Evil rises, God chooses a servant, saves out of the flood, and the clock is reset. I know you're familiar with that one." They smiled at each other again and Noah tried not to roll his eyes at the unavoidable pun.

Peter continued as if he were suddenly behind a pulpit in front of a large crowd. "Evil rises, God chooses a servant, one man of faith becomes the father of all who have faith, evil is purged from the promised land, leaving behind only a pillar of salt, and the clock is reset. Evil rises, God chooses a servant, brother becomes slave becomes ruler, famine fails to wipe out the line of salvation, and the clock is reset. Evil rises, God chooses a servant, captives are set free in the midst of pestilence and plague, and the clock is reset. Evil rises in kingdom after kingdom, but God establishes His everlasting Kingdom and time after time, the clock is reset. From Babylon to Persia to Greece to Rome to Nazi Germany to the rise of Islam seen in this very century . . . Time after time, the enemies of God rise to wipe out His people and His way, to set themselves up as gods of all they survey only to be snuffed like smoldering wicks as God resets the clock until He sees fit to do away with evil and all who cause it, once and for all . . . on His own timetable. Through it all, He calls and empowers His servants to be faithful and upright in the midst of a system that is faithless and corrupt. We are, right now, surrounded by a great cloud of witnesses to these things who testify that the war is already won because the King of kings is seated at the right hand of the very throne of God. We simply have to look with spiritual eyes. When you do learn to look through spiritual eyes, you will see that any battles still waging are merely the desperate last-ditch efforts of a defeated retreating horde . . . and all of the questions you are struggling with will quietly fade into eternity."

Noah was silent as he pondered what his friend had to say. He was humbled and a little ashamed that he had to be reminded of these things—things he already knew all too well in that deep place from which his recent dreams emanated. It was hard for him to see himself in the same vein as Abraham, Joseph, David, Daniel, and all the rest who were called to stand firm in the midst of the seemingly endless struggle, but he remembered that they were all ordinary men just like him. Men of faith just like him. Still, it was too much to consider. He felt so alone in the struggle, even after confiding in Martha and Peter. It was a strange feeling for him. He had spent a good part of his life alone while never really feeling alone. He preferred being alone, for the most part. There was something about this particular struggle that seemed to expose a repressed need for a companion, a thought he could not get away from, waking or sleeping.

As his thoughts returned to the disturbing dream he'd been having and the fact that he couldn't get away from it—even while wide awake and in the most loving and secure environment he knew—his face must have turned white again because Martha returned to her former demeanor of doting concern. She noticed as he finally drummed up the courage to look directly at the frame projecting the images of Ruth. "So you haven't even spoken to her?" she asked softly.

"I tried. I just couldn't . . . I didn't know what to say. I'm not even sure how to get in touch with her. That's why I'm here, I mean besides . . . you know . . . needing to discuss the Apocalypse and all." They all laughed as he made light of their serious discussion, then he looked Martha in the eye. "Is it too late? I mean, did I miss my chance?"

"Oh, honey . . . there's only one way to find out," Martha encouraged.

"Do you know where she is or how I can get in touch with her?" he asked sheepishly.

"Well, since she changed jobs we have to wait for her to contact us. Her link is no longer public. She hasn't been at liberty to tell us what her job is, but it apparently comes with an impenetrable wall of security. She throws us a card at Christmas and a short blurb every now and then, but I think she is too busy to get away to come see us. You're not the only one who gets lost every now and then," Martha said in a way that communicated how happy she was to see Noah and that she had the same hope for seeing Ruth.

"I really need to find her . . . I know that now more than anything." Noah's words trailed off into his empty stare toward the viewer. It looked as if he were staring right through it. He thought of the dream one last time and again decided against verbalizing it.

Martha spoke up again, "Perhaps your friend Dr. Abus could help you. He seems to be someone of quite importance. Don't you think he could cut through the red tape for you?"

"Well, he found me, didn't he?"

Martha took his hand again. "Ruthie is a pure and noble creature . . . I don't think she's capable of holding a grudge, but she is strong. Eventually she'll overcome any hurt and pain you may have caused her . . . that's only good for you if you're the one there for her when she does, so . . . I wouldn't waste any more time."

"Would it be okay if I *wasted* at least through dinner time and maybe a short night's rest in the guest bedroom?"

"I wouldn't have it any other way. What would you like for dinner, dear?"

Dinner was the best meal Noah could ever remember in his life, both for the home-cooked food and for the company. It had been far too long since he had experienced either. After dinner they talked some more, mostly about Noah's last two years alone, until Noah could sense that Martha was becoming fatigued. As he got up to excuse himself, Martha slowly resurrected from her recliner to show him to his room.

"Martha, sit back down. I'll make sure he's taken care of," Peter said with merciful firmness as he took her arm and helped her up, knowing that she would not relent.

"Oh, stop your doting," she replied with joyful stubbornness. "I can manage to walk down the hall of my own home."

"I know where everything is, sit back down, the two of ya," Noah said in the same pseudo-ornery tone.

"Don't be silly, I'm gonna make sure you're comfortable whether you're . . . well, *comfortable* with that or not!" They all laughed and made their way to the guest room at Martha's pace.

Martha very rarely went in that room, not just because of her trouble getting around but mostly because it reminded her of Ruth's absence. She made sure it was always ready to receive guests, as was their custom, but she did that by proxy. Peter was always more than willing and equal to the task. As she slowly made her way down the hall, she couldn't help but see, in her mind's eye, Ruthie, standing in the doorway with her bright smile and colorful cheeks.

Ruth was Martha's older sister's granddaughter. She lived with her grandmother for most of her childhood, so she got to know Peter and Martha quite well as they would visit from time to time. Ruth came from a broken home, if there were such a thing anymore. It was so common for people to have children together and then just move on to someone new as if it were nothing that her situation, sadly, wasn't out of the ordinary. That fact didn't erase the pain that Ruth and everyone else in that situation felt. The pain was real—they just didn't know where it was coming from. Society had been lied to for so long about what a *normal* family was that they completely disconnected the pain from its source. Eventually, both of Ruth's parents succumbed prematurely to substance abuse, quite separately of course but similarly—different vices, separate ways . . . same disease. Martha saw from the first moment Noah and Ruth sat across from one another at her Sunday dinner table that this would be an unspoken bond between the two. A strong bond that would either hold fast for a lifetime or be violently rent apart by its own, untamed energy. Martha was still praying for the former, even though, to all who knew them, it looked as if the latter had already happened.

After her grandmother passed, Ruth really had nowhere to go, although she was in college when it happened and pretty much on her own already, she still felt homeless and abandoned. The only reason she decided to go on to get her masters was to have an excuse to come and stay with Peter and Martha. They were delighted, of course. She never even applied to any other schools, just the one near their home, near what she now called home.

The very room they were all making their way toward had been Ruth's room for many years. Noah couldn't help but smile as he remembered all the times Martha shooed him out of there as she lectured him on how it was improper for him to be in a lady's bed chamber—a very eccentric and antiquated principle to the world they lived in but one he loved her for all the more.

As they filed though the bedroom door, it became a portal to even more memories of Ruth. This was hardest, of course, for Noah, but even Peter let out a wistful sigh as he turned on the lamp on the nightstand.

Noah immediately noticed that the picture was still there. The one she had always kept on her nightstand. The one picture she loved so much that she couldn't allow it to only exist in cyberspace, cycling through the slideshow of some digital picture frame as if it had no place to call its own. She had it printed onto a metallic photo-sheet and then framed with the wood from the walking stick she found the day the picture was taken. She had carved the inscription—*Wherever you go, I go*—into the wood across the top of the frame. It was something they used to say to each other in a flirtatious, pseudo-competitive manner while deciding how adventurous to get on their many rigorous hiking trips. It was nearly indestructible, the time capsule containing that perfect moment. The fact that she left it behind as she moved on with her life gave little hope to Noah that the perfect moment, itself, was as indestructible.

He picked it up as if it were some sort of talisman that would magically transport him back to that day. Strangely, he almost felt her head on his shoulder and her sun-lightened hair fall across his hand on her shoulder as depicted in the image. The feel of the walking stick they were both grasping when the picture was taken was real. He tightened his grip on the frame as he remembered how his fingers had randomly encountered the softness of the back side of her hand as they playfully fought over the enchanted staff, but no matter how tightly he gripped it, the warmth of her flesh could not be summoned out of the cold, rough, dead wood.

Ruth loved this picture. To anyone else, it was a picture of two young hikers in front of a waterfall—the waterfall being the subject of interest and beauty—but to Ruth, it was much more. Noah never really liked the picture all that much himself because Ruth's hair had blown into her face, concealing all but one eye and a sun-touched cheek. Noah never knew that the reason he didn't like it was the very reason Ruth loved it. It concealed her . . . covered her . . . but revealed him as she saw him, a wise and valiant protector. The way he pulled her in with an irresistible arm and placed his cheek on the top of her head with meekness, it made her feel wanted, needed, and safe. That feeling did not last, however. Noah's emotional self-preservation eventually interfered with the heroic picture she had painted of him and leaving the photo behind when she moved turned it into an icon of his fall.

Noah had lost all consciousness that Peter and Martha were even in the room until Martha spoke up softly, "You can have that if you want, dear."

Noah snapped back to the present. "I . . ." He wanted to say that he couldn't, but the words just wouldn't form.

"Don't you worry about it, dear. It's not ours anyway . . . if anyone has rights to it, you do."

Peter stayed wisely silent while he placed a firm hand on Noah's shoulder. He was going to give him the rundown on where to find everything he needed for the night's stay, but instead he gave his shoulder a squeeze then ushered Martha out with a nod.

"Thank you . . . thank you both . . . for everything."

As the door closed gingerly behind them, Noah collapsed in both physical and emotional exhaustion, face-first onto the foot of the bed. As he took in a deep breath for the purpose of letting out a cleansing sigh, memories of Ruth came flowing to his brain with the air now being filtered through the bedspread. Maybe he was still reliving the image in the photograph, imagining his face gently pressed against the top of her head or maybe he still had his jungle-sharpened senses, but he could swear he could smell the sweet scent of her hair as he took in that first deep breath with his face buried in the bed. A crystal-clear image of Ruth came to him as he remembered how she would often lie on top of the bedspread with her head toward the foot of the bed and her feet on the wall above her pillows as she studied or read. Noah didn't even get up to turn off the light, nor did he right himself in the bed to crawl between the sheets. He muttered softly, "Wherever you go, I go," then fell into a deep sleep right there, smothered in Ruth's lingering presence.

As was his habit, Peter prayerfully patrolled the house. Well into the night, he saw that the light was still on, so he poked his head in to see if everything was okay. He found the young adventurer with the tropical tan shivering in the North American night. Peter quietly pulled one of Martha's home-crafted afghans from the chair in the corner and placed it over him meekly then turned out the light and retired himself.

Noah slept like a baby under their peaceful protection, without disturbance while awake or asleep. He seemed to be cured of his reoccurring dream, at least for now. The pleasantly painful memories of Ruth now overpowered the disturbing, chaotic scene that had been haunting him. What used to be a fleeting glimpse of her that faded into the sea of tortured humanity was now a portrait over the hearth of his memories.

The next morning came too soon for any of them. Noah took what Peter and Martha had to say to heart and he really didn't want to waste any more time, so he got an early start. As they were embracing and prolonging the goodbye, Peter called Noah's attention to a box by the door.

"I hope you can carry this okay wherever it is you're going. I know you don't have a vehicle, but I'd really like you to take it."

"What is it?" Noah said, a little caught off guard.

"It's just some books, you know, those ancient things with pages made from paper."

"What, no papyrus or clay tablets?" Noah joked as he removed the lid to take a look inside.

"I'm not that old." They both laughed to cover the uncomfortable feeling that comes with personal gift-giving between two men with such respect for one another.

"Oh Peter . . . I can't take these." The box was full of Peter's own personal copies of the Scriptures in the original languages along with some other key study tools and an electronic copy of the entirety of Peter's own writings. He also threw in some primary source history books and an antique, leather-bound copy of *Robinson Crusoe* for enjoyment.

"If you're called to . . ." Peter couldn't finish his sentence. Both he and Martha became emotional at the thought of never seeing him again. ". . . there's no better place for them than with you."

"Thank you . . ." Noah could get no more out than that and since he couldn't offer them any solace, he thought it best to turn and leave after giving Martha one last kiss on the cheek.

He placed the picture frame in the box and started on his way. They watched him carry the heavy burden down the sidewalk toward the Mag-Lev station until he was out of sight, then they closed the door behind him and began their morning prayer time. There was but one subject of their petitions this morning—two if one could count Ruth Evans as a separate subject . . . they did not.

CHAPTER SEVEN

As he often did after dinner, to digest and watch the news, Yafeu had just eased himself to the floor and reclined with his head resting against the bottom of the couch when his youngest son, an energetic five, came running around the end of the couch and pounced on him as five-year-olds do.

"Hodari . . . No! No! Papa just ate . . . you're going to burst me like a bubble." Yafeu laughed as he tickled the little attacker.

"But Mutegi is chasing me again . . . you have to protect me!" he replied through uncontrollable laughter.

"If he comes here, I will tickle him too . . . just like this." Yafeu continued tickling until the child could barely breathe. When he could stand it no longer, the child wriggled out of reach like a harmless baby snake. Yafeu was too worn out to move from his reclining position, so he turned his attention back to the WNN.

The Network was again doing a story on the Babel Resurgence Project, so Yafeu increased the volume on his implant to overcome the noise of the other children playing and the baby crying. His wife sat on the couch behind him and started nursing the baby. As the baby calmed down and settled into the nourishing comfort of her mother's embrace, Dalila reached down in front of her and massaged Yafeu's scalp tenderly with the tips of her fingers. She knew that it was hard for him to watch the reports about the Project but that he also couldn't help himself. He had strived so hard to get on the Project and when he was demoted to ground duty she noticed a quiet but despondent change in him. She wanted to tell him she was worried about him, but she felt that voicing her concern may only make things worse for him. He felt an uncommonly strong protective instinct over her and the children and to tell him that he was worrying her would only make him feel worse. So she quietly energized him with her loving and protective touch.

"Yes, Bob, that's right. When fully provisioned, *Epoch Utopia* will be a microcosm of the Earth. She will have oceans, seen here in blue around the outside . . . the very outer layer of the living sections. She will have forests . . . scattered throughout the living area, seen here in green. And she will have farmland also seen here scattered throughout the living areas . . . depicted by the brown color here on the model."

Dr. Sorenson was interrupted by Bob bringing the conversation back around to the first of the three subjects, "When you say oceans, do you mean salt water with sea life in them?"

"Actually, yes . . . two of the four outer levels on each section will have salt water with specimens from Earth's ocean living and hopefully, thriving in them. The other two outer levels on each section will be fresh water. Some for fresh water life and some for the needs of the crew. There will, of course, be plenty of hydrogen and oxygen stored here in the micro gravity environment of the center engineering section. So if the need for more water arises, they will have the ability to simply create it as a by-product of the fuel cell power plants." As Dr. Sorenson continued, little Hodari cuddled up next to his father on the floor, satisfied that he was too distracted to tickle him anymore.

"One more thing about the water, Bob. Although the vessel will have quite a strong magnetic field surrounding it when it is in motion, the layer of water on the outer decks will help to protect the crew from the harmful radiation they will encounter as they travel through space."

Bob interjected, "Really . . . a water radiation shield?"

"That's right, Bob . . . they're not completely dependent on that, but it is certainly an intentional design meant to aid in the radiation shielding."

"Won't the fish and other sea life be in danger?" Bob asked with the pseudo concern of a news anchor man.

"Well, only if all the other shielding methods fail and that's not likely to happen. And also . . . not all of the water-bound life will be represented in the tanks themselves. There will be genome samples of every living thing on Earth safely stored away in cryostasis. If they need some more fish . . . they'll just grow them."

"Very interesting, Dr. Sorenson. We'll hear more about some of the other micro-ecosystems on the vessel later, but for right now let's move on to the status of the construction and provisioning. How is everything going?"

"Things are right on schedule. In fact, they have already started shuttling things aboard. The gravity simulation seems to be working fine and the sections seem to be communicating as planned—no hiccups yet . . ."

As Dr. Sorenson continued on, Yafeu mumbled, not quite under his breath, and pulled his little one close, as if protecting him from ignorance and arrogance. "They won't be communicating much longer if they don't re-path the secondaries like I told them . . ." He was now almost yelling at the viewer, "No hiccups my—" He realized that his young children were watching him, so he tried to tame his language and demeanor. "On schedule! Not if you count all the re-work necessary because of all the substandard installs . . ."

He would have yammered on and on if it were not for his wife's calming presence, "Calm down, Yafeu . . ." she said in a hushed tone, "there is nothing you can do about it. You did your part. The responsibility is theirs now."

With those words still hanging in the air, Yafeu received an incoming message prompt on his implant and because his implant was mastering the viewer at the moment, the communication ID appeared across the bottom.

SPACE ADMINISTRATION – OFFICE OF ENGINEERING MANAGEMENT

They both sat straight up in surprise and fought the urge to look around as if someone were eavesdropping on their conversation.

"Dalila, the children . . . please . . ." Yafeu stood to his feet and patted Hodari on the behind as if shooing a cow out of the garden.

"Come children, let's play outside . . . shhh . . . quietly so Papa can hear, okay? Come on." Dalila took Hodari by the hand while holding the baby in the other and herded the whole family out to the backyard. Hodari shook free just long enough to grab the soccer ball from the shelf by the door and flash Papa one last smile, hoping that he would follow.

Yafeu waited for the door to close behind them and then gave the answer command. "Hello . . ."

There was a slight pause while the video image loaded to the viewer overtop the WNN broadcast. A uniformed man appeared on the viewer and spoke in an intentional tone, "Mr. Amadi?"

"Yes . . . how may I help you?" Yafeu recognized the uniform as the new standard designed for the Engineering Corp of *Epoch Utopia*. The man's face was also vaguely familiar, but in that split second he couldn't recall who it was for sure.

"Well, I'm hoping we may be able to help each other. I'm not interrupting anything, am I?" the man said, trying to get right to the point while still being polite.

"No . . . not at all . . . I was just enjoying a little family time," Yafeu said, trying not to sound nervous or too eager to please.

"Well, I don't want to keep you from that . . . I know you spend a lot of time away from home. Let me get right to it so I can let you go."

"It's not a problem . . . really . . . I'm happy to talk . . . Mr? ahh . . ."

"Oh, I'm sorry . . . I'm Dietrich Keller Chief Engineer, *Epoch Utopia.*"

"No, I'm sorry, Chief. I thought I recognized you, but I couldn't see your rank insignia and I didn't want to assume . . . actually, you kind of caught me off guard. I never expected to get a call from you personally, sir." Yafeu stumbled over his words wondering what was behind this great honor.

"Chief will do just fine . . . we'll leave 'sir' to the command crew."

"How may I be of service, Chief?" Yafeu replied, a little set at ease by the vocabulary of fraternity.

"Well, Mr. Amadi, I'd like to see if you could come in to headquarters for an interview."

"Of course." Yafeu didn't know whether to be excited or nervous. There were two types of interviews in his field. One could be good and one could be very bad.

The Chief saw on Yafeu's face the dilemma in his head. "I'm sorry . . . a job interview," he reassured him. "I'm not on any fault-finding mission or anything, at least not where you're concerned. You have nothing to worry about. Though there has been a series of technical failures on the Project. While investigating them I came across records of your communications with your supervisor and the recommendation report you attempted to pass up the chain. I'm embarrassed to say that if the supervisors had listened to your recommendations we would not have had the failures we did. I apologize for your recent demotion . . . I'd like to make it up to you."

"Thank you, Si . . . ahh, Chief. Please . . . no need to apologize." Yafeu was dumbfounded by the Chief's honesty. It was very refreshing in a field where blame was passed around like a hot potato. He found himself respecting the Chief immensely.

"I'll be on the surface tomorrow by 12:00 p.m. Earth Standard Time. Come to my office and we'll talk about it in detail. Okay?"

"Yes, certainly . . . I'll see you tomorrow and thank you again." The viewer returned to the news broadcast after a nod from the Chief.

Yafeu ran to the backyard, intercepted a pass of the soccer ball between siblings, and dribbled it to the end of the yard. With a powerful kick the ball hit the back of the net and Yafeu's arms shot into the air as he jumped and yelled, "Goooaaalll!" The whole family swarmed him and almost knocked him over as if he had just won the World Cup and that is exactly how he felt.

"Who was that, Yafeu?" Dalila shouted over the celebration.

"It was the chief engineer himself!" he exclaimed joyously while grabbing up as many of the children as possible and bursting into laughter. He spun them around until they all ended up in a big pile on the lawn.

"Well, what did he want?" she asked, unable to keep a serious face in all the commotion. She was very happy to see him come alive again.

"He asked me to come to his office tomorrow . . . he wants to talk about my ideas!" he yelled as he sat up with children rolling off him like drops of rain.

"Are you sure? I mean . . . he said that?" She was trying not to sound worried, but the last time he was called to the office, so to speak, he was demoted.

"Yes, yes . . . he's offering me a job."

"A job? What job?"

"I'll tell you later . . . who wants ice cream?"

All five of the older children cheered some version of "me . . . me!" or "I do . . . me too!" while jumping up and down or raising a hand high so Papa would see. Yafeu shot Dalila a mischievous smile with eyes that rolled in purposeful avoidance and feigned innocence as he herded the children into the house with orders to wash up.

"Yafeu Agymah!" she scolded while chasing after him as best as she could with a baby on the hip. "Don't you give me that! What's going on?"

"Don't worry, Dalila, I'll tell you everything as soon as I return from the capital."

"What . . . when?"

"I have to leave tonight. He wants to see me in his office tomorrow afternoon. I'm not sure when I'll be back."

"Well, what can you tell me now?" she said impatiently. She was not looking forward to his leaving tonight and she certainly could not stand waiting until he got back for the details.

"I told you already, he wants to offer me a job," he said, playfully holding back any new details until he saw the lioness that he both loved and feared start to come out in her expression. "They had some system failures after I left and during his investigation he came across all the reports and recommendations I tried to pass up the chain. He actually apologized for my demotion and said he wanted to make it up to me."

That was enough to tame the charging lioness into an embrace instead of the playful slap on the shoulder she had first intended. "Oh Yafeu, that's so wonderful."

He pulled her in tight with all his newfound strength, kissed the baby on the head, and then lingered long on her lips until the younger children started giggling and making noises of playful disgust. The oldest daughter, Kioni, who was twelve, turned away in actual disgust and headed out the door while mumbling something about that being just what she needed to see before eating.

"Mmmmm . . ." They both moaned loudly before breaking the kiss, just to egg on the children.

"Last one out the door has to give me a bite of theirs . . ." As Yafeu gave this playful ultimatum, the children sprung into action and raced for the door knowing that he was serious about following through with the threat and that his bites were very big.

Dalila was last out the door as always. As much because of the habit of herding them from behind as because of the heavy but welcome burden on her hip and all the paraphernalia that goes along with having one still in diapers. At this point in her life she would feel naked without a baby on her hip. After six, it was no burden at all, really. She was able to go just about anywhere and do just about anything as if the baby on her hip was simply an extension of herself. She tried not to think about the ramifications of Yafeu's application for crew status on *Epoch Utopia* and what that would mean for their family, present and future. That was not today's worry, but with the call from the Chief Engineer himself, the day of that worry did seem much closer to her now.

The children all turned and pointed at her as she closed the door behind her and yelled some version of "Mama's last, Papa's gonna eat your ice cream." They were all quite relieved that they themselves would have their own ice cream all to themselves. Of course, they did. Yafeu knew she was always the last one out of the house and that the trick would still work on the children, regardless. He did take a large bite of her serving of what passed as ice cream just to keep his future threats believable, but he had always taken large bites of her food since way before any of the children were born. It was one of his very first flirtatious attempts when they first met. Her reaction to it has never changed. A pseudo-angry use of his name as if it were a curse word followed by a playful slap on the shoulder. It was all an act on both sides because they both knew that he would never let her go hungry, no matter what the cost.

He slowly enjoyed what had been served to him as he sat quietly and watched his family as if he were looking at a nostalgic snapshot in a photo album that recorded nothing but a hopeful future for them. The ice cream itself was not much more than a poor attempt at chemically reproducing the experience of real ice cream, but it melted in the heat of an African evening all the same. The children had never known real ice cream, so they were more than content with the treat. Yafeu coveted their childhood innocence and was determined to protect it for as long as possible. His one fear was that somehow their childhood might be stolen from them as his was from him. This fear made it even more important to him that he make crew status. He wanted to take them all away from here to a place he knew would be stable always. No one knew what kind of chaos the world might fall into once the Supreme Ruler disembarked on *Epoch Utopia* never to return again. True, he was leaving his son behind to rule in his stead, but history was full of sons who have failed to live up to the legacy left to them by their fathers. There was too much of a chance that the world would break into its preassembled pieces once he was gone and that the wars of his childhood would visit his children in theirs. Yafeu was determined to save them from that.

The course of that determination found him kissing each one on the forehead as they were put down for the night in their beds before he again left them behind in search of their future. Dalila tried to convince him to stay until morning, but with a loving embrace he explained that he had to overcome the time change between their home and the capital and that he had very little margin as it was. He held her longer than either one could stand without feeling the temptation of further intimacy, but they both found the strength to let go as they had so many times before. Yafeu turned, shouldered his on-call bag, and headed for the door.

"You are my African Queen . . ." he declared as he walked away with his head turned toward her and his eyes locked upon hers.

". . . and you are my Mighty Hunter . . ." she answered back as always. "Call me as soon as you know anything more," she said with renewed excitement about the reason for his impending absence.

"I will. I love you," he whispered through the closing door.

"I love you . . ." she said to the closed door with a hopeful sigh that exclaimed her determination to enjoy the empty room as a temporary place of peace and quiet and not as a lonely lover's wallow.

As Yafeu traveled, his thoughts slowly migrated from his wife and children to the business at hand. As he wondered how much of the information he had attempted to pass up the chain actually reached the Chief, he pulled his electronic pad from his bag to review it for himself. Luckily, he had not been completely cut off from the Project with his demotion or he would have lost any security clearance to access the records and reports. It was against policy to download them to any personal device and even though he had the technical knowhow to make unauthorized copies, he needed his job much too much to risk getting caught. The fact that his original compositions were created on his own device and then uploaded to the Project server was a technical loophole he often utilized as an insurance policy. When his supervisor or someone else up the chain tried to bury evidence of their incompetence, at the very least, Yafeu had the original copies of his own reports.

As he started reading through his records, he found that many of the logs and reports that he specifically referenced were no longer present on the Project server. He wasn't surprised, but it made him wonder how the Chief came across the information. The files weren't restricted or archived; they were just missing. It was obvious that someone was trying to cover their tracks and who would they be hiding the info from if it were not the Chief? This would remain just as much a mystery to Yafeu as it was to the Chief.

A few days ago, a man with Palace credentials marched into the Chief's office, slid a data storage device across his desk, and then sat, staring at him coldly while he accessed the information. It was not only the files that Yafeu had discovered missing but all of his reports and recommendations as well as recordings of conversations he had had with his supervisor. They were all organized and categorized as if Yafeu himself had put the collection together in order to make his case before a review board. There was information in there that Yafeu could not have possibly had access to, but when the Chief asked where it came from, the man simply told him to "fix it," in no uncertain terms.

This was not the first time the Project had been put back on track by a mysterious man or Three. Because the Project was the Supreme Ruler's first priority, gathering and analyzing intel on those involved was the Three's first priority. The Chief was smart enough to know that it would be wise to simply make use of the information instead of questioning further its origins. Accidents were known to happen to those who question too much or who were simply too incompetent to forgive. He didn't want to find himself floating off into space in a malfunctioning craft with a slowly depleting oxygen supply or find himself burning up upon reentry because of a faulty heat shield. The space program had long ago conquered the technology to safely travel in and out of the Earth's atmosphere yet these accidents still happened from time to time . . . but only to the right people.

Chief Keller immediately set about the task of verifying the validity of the data, using his engineer's mind to filter out the fear that accompanies a visit from "Them." There wasn't even a name for the department or agency or bureau . . . or whatever the organizational structure was that they belonged to. Their existence was known only to those who were high enough up in the administration of a Palace project and, like Keller, had had the unfortunate pleasure of a visit from one. They were known only as "Them." The enigmatic "They" referred to in a whispered statement such as, "be careful . . . they're listening."

It wasn't long before the Chief was able to identify the major causes of the recent system failures now that he had Yafeu's reports. He took a trip to the site and found things just as Yafeu had described. Keller interrogated Yafeu's immediate supervisor and though he found him to be borderline incompetent and slow to pass Yafeu's concerns up the chain, he did eventually pass some of the information on to his superior, so Keller merely busted him to tech instead of firing him. The ironic thing was that the only reason he passed it up was to keep Yafeu from pestering him. It was Yafeu's competence and persistence that saved his job even after he had busted Yafeu to ground duty.

Behind his stoic expression, Keller was seething inside and wanted to fire everyone in sight, but he knew he had a timetable to keep, so he couldn't afford to lose the only people with intricate knowledge of the systems of *Epoch Utopia* . . . especially after the personnel losses of the Mars incident. There was one person he was going to fire for sure, the middle manager who failed to take action on Yafeu's information. The missing files and other fingerprints of a cover-up could be traced to him, but when Keller went to confront him, the middle manager was also missing. The story was that after the system failures, he knew he was liable, so he covered his tracks as best he could and then got nervous and bailed. Keller knew it is impossible for someone with an implant to "disappear" on their own. His own visit from "Them" confirmed his inner, never spoken suspicions that "They" had already taken care of the matter.

Once Keller was satisfied that he had left no stone unturned in his investigation of the system failures, he set about the task of repairing not only the physical plant of *Epoch Utopia* but the systemic personnel problems in the technical crew. The chasm between management and the technicians was like the Grand Canyon. He knew he had to bridge the gap and the only way to do it was to put someone into leadership who had a passion for the Project, an intricate knowledge of the systems, and a healthy respect for the big picture—someone who was not stuck in his own box and at the same time knew the reasons why others were. After carefully reading all of Yafeu's reports, Keller saw him as that man. More importantly, he thought that "They," whoever "They" were, thought that as well. If Keller didn't implement Yafeu's recommendations, then he was risking a mysterious disappearance of his own. He would go one better and make Yafeu implement his own recommendations. It was an old leadership technique he had learned long ago . . . delegate a task to the one who suggested it and two things will happen: the task will be carried out with the passion of ownership, and there will be fewer suggestions from those who would rather complain than take responsibility.

Keller was so convinced that Yafeu was the man for the job that he contacted him immediately. He didn't wait for a committee meeting or even until he returned to his office on the ground. He wanted Yafeu there waiting for him when he returned from *Epoch Utopia* so as not to waste another instant. There really was no time to lose. The Supreme Ruler was immoveable when it came to the departure date—immoveable on anything, really—but especially on this point. He was a man obsessed . . . a very powerful man obsessed. Even the rail launchers were not fast enough to keep up with the acceleration of his insanity.

Yafeu looked out the window as his flight approached the Space Administration complex just outside the capital. The rail launchers had always fascinated him and he enjoyed watching them in action, especially from the air. When he first started on the Project, it took an enormous amount of time and rocket fuel to shuttle the workers and materials to and from the site. Since the completion of the launchers, the flight time and the prep time between flights had been dramatically reduced and the need for fuel had been reduced to the demands of navigation only. The escape velocity of the shuttles was now achieved by literally hurling them into space with a modified railgun. From the launch station, it did not seem as if they were being launched into space but just off into the horizon. The rails were tens of kilometers long and they held an almost absolute line, not following the curvature of the Earth. In this way, they could reach great velocity without having to directly counteract the full force of Earth's gravity at any one moment. It was almost like boarding a train to space. The drone shuttles were programmed to launch with the greatest rate of acceleration the particular cargo in their payload would allow for, while the personnel shuttles were given a governor to ensure that no one's nose ended up in the back of his skull. Yafeu loved to watch a drone shuttle full of something dense, like ore, or a non-compressible fluid, disappear in an instant from the rail launcher only to see another roll in and replace it like rounds in an automatic artillery piece. One would think that the denser the load, the slower the vehicle as it moved off the launcher, but quite the opposite was true. The more dense the payload, the less affected it was by the tendency to distort or denature under the extreme g-forces, thus the more energy could be applied to it in a shorter span of time. That energy was almost limitless because it was provided by a stationary nuclear power plant at the launch site. The concept was quite simple, really. A series of electro-magnetic fields fired off in succession down the length of the rails opposing the opposite polarity being generated by the launch vehicle and thus propelling it up the rails and off into space. Since the power plant did not have to be carried on the launch vehicle itself, the vehicles were much lighter than previous methods of achieving orbit with more room for cargo. The personnel transports did have to use some of the cargo space for extra fuel since humans and other life-forms being ferried to *Epoch Utopia* could not survive the extreme acceleration necessary to achieve escape velocity from the launcher alone. When there were people or other fragile cargo aboard, the rail launcher was utilized more like the steam catapult of an old-style military aircraft carrier. It assisted the onboard engines as much as it could without killing anyone or anything. A last-minute, high-altitude firing of the escape rockets was what ultimately achieved orbit for the vehicle at a safe rate of acceleration for those aboard.

The rail launchers Yafeu was looking at now in wonder were the first of many constructed around the world for the purpose of provisioning *Epoch Utopia* with all the earthly things she would need to be a home away from home. Every other method of launching cargo into space that had been utilized since the start of the Project was still in use as well. The Palace was pushing such a demanding schedule that the Space Administration could not afford to retire any of the outdated technologies. They had every available space plane and rocket launch pad in the world ferrying cargo to *Epoch Utopia* and they still were not planning to have her fully provisioned by the time she departed for the six-month test flight.

Beside the pure necessity of using every available technology, a dramatic rocket launch was seen as nostalgic and traditional by the Supreme Ruler and could be more easily surrounded by pomp and circumstance because of its raw power and self-induced fireworks show . . .tailor-made for a good PR campaign. The rail launchers were impressive to those, like Yafeu, who understood the monumental technological feat of a controlled rail gun burst, but the launch itself was short-lived, almost instantaneous—and apart from the sonic boom and the seemingly disappearing vehicle, there was no display of raw power and no fireworks. There was tremendous power, but it was hidden to those who did not have eyes to see, or ears to hear.

The hidden power of the rail launchers was something that Sargon was content to keep hidden and out of the limelight. When the program first went operational, there had been several incidents of miscalculation resulting in many deaths. A slight error in measuring the mass or density of a payload could and often did result in an over accelerated launch, leaving everyone aboard crushed to death under their own weight. This was not known to the public nor would it be. When the casualties started to be missed by their friends and loved ones, a mysterious man with Palace credentials would show up with a cover story. Since then, governors were installed on the personnel shuttles in an attempt to ensure that they would never accelerate faster than the human body could endure, but it was not a foolproof solution. There was just too much energy involved, the control of which was an illusion.

As a technician on the Project, Yafeu was launched in this manner on a regular basis, and he had no fear of it, but he did have his suspicions about the dangers. There was one occasion he could remember that felt odd to him and he always wondered about it. They were expecting a shuttle full of their duty relief, but when it arrived, he and the other techs were told they had to pull double duty, no questions asked. He happened to be working in the main engineering bay when the shuttle was guided in by a work pod. He thought it was odd that a personnel shuttle was being docked in the engineering section in the first place, but when he noticed that the call letters on the side were the same as the ones on his travel orders for later that day he knew something was not right. He knew some of the techs on that duty cycle. He never saw or heard from them again after that day. It was a feeling he knew he was going to have to get used to if he achieved crew status, so he didn't let it consume him. After losing his family and especially his little brother in the wars, he developed a very calloused corner of his mind where he could shove painful or fearful thoughts and memories. In a man bent on evil, this could be a very dangerous trait, but in Yafeu it manifested as courage.

As his flight landed, Yafeu took one last look at the rail launchers and wondered how soon it would be before he felt the rush of being hurled into space once again, then he regathered his thoughts for the important meeting he was about to have. His flight arrived in plenty of time for him to make it over to the Chief's office before noon, but he felt like he was late. His legs could not outrun the urgency he felt in the pit of his stomach. He made it to the office with plenty of time to spare, leaving him nothing to do but sit and wait—a practice he did not excel at. This was all too evident to the receptionist outside Chief Keller's office who found that even seemingly constant updates on the Chief's location could not quell the tension in the air. Yafeu was a man of action and great energy and it was often disturbing for people of more laid-back personality types to be around him for any length of time. This was usually not a problem because he didn't often stay in one place very long, but today he had no choice.

After what seemed to be an eternity, Chief Keller burst through the door of the reception area. He was a man of average height for a northern European, with a build that seemed to overcompensate for the loss of muscle mass one experiences after many trips into space. As he whisked by the desk to check for messages on his way through, Yafeu sprung to his feet behind the Chief, causing the receptionist to point to him with great relief. Keller spun around and welcomed him heartily.

"Mr. Amadi! So glad you could make it on such short notice."

Yafeu was instantly put at ease by the Chief's enthusiasm and found himself instinctually offering his hand for a handshake before it occurred to him that maybe he should be saluting instead. As his military-style haircut betrayed, Keller was used to being saluted, but he returned Yafeu's gesture before the moment became awkward, continuing to put him at ease.

Yafeu sputtered out clumsily, "No problem at all . . . thank you for . . . having me"—as if the Chief were having him over for dinner or something.

Keller responded with a simple nod and then ushered him into the office and offered him a seat. As he sat himself, he opened a small door under his desk and grabbed two bottles of cold water. He tossed one over to Yafeu, catching him slightly by surprise.

"Flying always makes me thirsty. I'm sure you're a little parched too." Before Yafeu could answer or thank him, Keller moved on in his polite but straight-to-the-point manner. "How would you like to be back aboard *Epoch Utopia*, Mr. Amadi?"

Yafeu almost choked on his first swig from the bottle as he was a little too eager to answer the question. "Yes, of course . . . yes . . . there is nothing I would like more, sir . . . I mean . . . Chief. Thank you, Chief Keller."

"Don't thank me yet. There's a few details we have to work out yet and . . . well . . . she's a real mess right now. I have a feeling you'll be cursing me soon, not thanking me." Keller laughed with a dry, humorless laugh.

"What can I do to help with the details?" Yafeu ignored the latter since he was unsure of the level of humor intended.

"Well, you'll just need to sign some things for the transfer, but that's not what I mean." Keller looked up with steely eyes and a stern German expression. "There will be no going around me."

"Chief?" Yafeu feigned ignorance.

Keller cracked a sly, knowing smile and snickered slightly. "You know what I'm talking about. You answer straight to me. I promise to always give you a fair hearing, but if I make a call that you don't agree with . . . there will be no second chances this time."

"A fair hearing is all I was ever looking for, Chief, and . . . not to sound obsequious, but I believe I will get it from you if you would be gracious enough to have an open-door policy with me."

Yafeu sounded sincere, so Keller lost the stone-faced expression and reassured him of his own sincerity. "I don't think we'll have a problem, but I can't have my management team questioning my calls once all the info is in and the debate is over."

Yafeu was confused for a moment, "How do you think my supervisor . . . and his supervisor for that matter, are going to react to me having a direct line to you?"

"You misunderstand, Mr. Amadi . . . you're not going to have a supervisor, well besides me. I mean you will be the supervisor—first level. I want you at the management committee meetings, and your proposals—that were so unfortunately ignored—I want you to implement them throughout all the tech teams."

Yafeu was uncharacteristically dumbfounded. He finally managed to verify that he had heard correctly. "First level?" That was three levels higher than he was when he left. It was, in fact, a professional engineer position normally.

"That's right. I want you to be in on the engineer meetings so you can be the ambassador of the big picture to the tech supervisors and technicians sand, quite frankly, help me to talk some sense into these know-it-all engineers on the management and planning committee."

"I'm very honored, sir. I'll give it everything I've got," he said enthusiastically while still feeling unequal to the task. "There's just one thing . . ." Yafeu paused to self-edit, not wanting to blow the tremendous opportunity he had just been given.

"What is it?" the Chief asked, sensing that Yafeu was a little overwhelmed.

"I'll give it my best shot—the ambassador to the techs thing—but in the past, many of them, well . . . they haven't exactly taken kindly to my . . . enthusiasm. I think they were threatened by it."

"Apparently for good reason: you're now their boss. Now they have no choice but to be inspired by it." Keller encouraged, "I've found that there are two types of leaders: the kind that get out in front on their own, and the kind that have had some label placed on them from some outside authority. The former are always actual leaders and the latter, not necessarily. The former very often face the petty opposition of the less industrious singlehandedly while the latter enjoy the double-edged sword of an official authority structure of rewards and punishments. The first has to truly lead with results while the second may get away with, for a while anyways, slave driving or bribery. I'm of the belief that if one were to marry the industriousness of the former with the official position of the latter, great things can happen. What I'm trying to say is that you have nothing to worry about. You will have gained the respect and the ear of many who were . . . threatened, as you say. And if some of them don't come around, well . . . you will now have the authority to do something about it. I think you will find that quite liberating. I'm sure there was a lot of frustration involved in being out in front but not having the authority to plant your flag in the undiscovered country, so to speak."

"I'm afraid you are seeing right through me, Chief. I feel like you just summed up the last few years of my life in a few sentences."

"Well, I'm glad to hear that I'm reading you right. I find it very important to get to know and understand one's crewmates. After all, we will be spending the rest of our lives together."

Yafeu choked on his water again as he tried desperately to ask the knee-jerk question that the Chief's last statement invoked. "Crew status?" He sat up straight and spilled some of the water down his shirt as if it were his first time drinking from a bottle.

"That's what you wanted, isn't it?" the Chief asked, knowing the answer but covering all his bases like a true engineer. "Did I misread your intentions?"

"No, no . . . I mean yes, that's what I want . . . it's just that the last twelve hours have been such a whirlwind. One moment I'm watching my career rocket away without me while I'm pulling ground duty and the next I'm in charge of the whole bloody tech team. To be honest, I've been so focused on the construction phase that official crew status didn't enter into my mind as the topic of our conversation. I'm just caught off guard but pleasantly . . . well, ecstatically surprised."

"We can't take everyone involved in the construction process, but it only makes sense that we try to recruit those who are closest to the Project and who know her best, *Epoch Utopia*, that is." The Chief gave Yafeu this off-handed compliment as he saw he wasn't taking any of this for granted. The Chief was really impressed by Yafeu's attitude and passion for the Project even as it made its way out into the open through clumsy stuttering and unfortunate dribbling.

"Thank you again, Chief Keller. I won't let you down," Yafeu said in a more composed manner as he recalibrated his mind to the new context of the conversation.

"I'm sure you won't, Amadi." The Chief cracked a habitual forced smile before he continued. "We've still got a lot to work out though, you and me . . . there are a few things in your recommendations and reports that I take issue with and we will have to hammer that all out before you go hog wild with the tech teams."

"Not a problem, Chief, I'm most anxious to hear your critique and any ideas you may have to help me to transition into such an overwhelming role," Yafeu said, mindful that there were probably going to be some hard conversations ahead.

The Chief sat silently for a moment, making Yafeu a little uncomfortable. He couldn't tell if the interview was over or if the Chief was just processing all the errors in Yafeu's understanding of the systems of *Epoch Utopia* to decide which one to correct him on first. Then, out of the blue, a sudden change in direction.

"I see here that you are quite the family man, Mr. Amadi," the Chief said to lighten the mood a little before dropping the hammer on the last, most difficult subject of conversation.

"Six beautiful children and a lovely wife of sixteen years," Yafeu replied with an unavoidable smile.

His smile waned as the Chief broached the next subject, "You know there are, well . . . limits, right?"

"Limits?" Yafeu asked, knowing he was not going to like the answer.

"You know . . . limits on the number of children per couple in the departing population, not to mention the strict rules on who will be allowed to marry whom in coming generations and how many children they'll be allowed to have. Population control is necessarily a top priority. If it gets out of control, it could mean the death of us all," Keller said with a stoic expression.

"I understand, I understand." Yafeu managed to utter in spite of the sick feeling in the pit of his stomach. Surely they knew his family situation when they decided to offer him the position. "Where does that leave me?" he asked softly.

"Well . . . the ideal is two children per couple. That is standard, stable replacement population. They're allowing up to four per couple, knowing that life is not ideal, but I have to be honest with you, six is really pushing it. I think you really need to prepare yourself for some hard decisions." For the first time, Keller did not look Yafeu straight in the eye.

"What decisions?" Yafeu said in the lion-like tone that emerged when he sensed a threat to his family. Certainly, they would not have the gall to ask him to leave behind his children or to choose between them somehow.

"Well, first and foremost, if you are even going to accept the offer under these uncertain circumstances . . . and secondly, if it comes down to it, do you leave some loved ones behind?" Keller kept talking quickly to cut off any emotional outburst that may ruin any chance of continuing the interview in a professional manner. "We all are going to have to do it at some level. We are all leaving behind parents and siblings and—yes, in some cases—children. I'm not saying that there are any definite requirements of you at this time, but you need to be aware of the seriousness of the decision you're making."

Yafeu sat in silence, knowing that his tone and speech could very easily get away from him. His gaze, however, did not leave the Chief's eyes, though they did not return the challenge.

"I think we've covered enough for today," the Chief said, physically rattled by the intense stare from the other side of the desk. "Go home, think about it . . . take your time . . . in fact, take a week of paid vacation . . . I'll take care of it. We'll talk in a week."

"Okay" was the only thing Yafeu could manage to say without losing it. He slowly stood up and walked out with his shoulders hunched uncharacteristically. *How dare he suggest . . .* Yafeu could not even finish the thought. Of all his many journeys, as a refugee through war-torn Africa and even to space and back, the journey home that day was the longest: for he carried a burden that even the weightlessness of space could not relieve.

CHAPTER EIGHT

The ride to the university was much shorter than Noah remembered. He didn't have time to successfully plan out his reunion with Rajen, so he would just have to let it play out on its own. He knew that Rajen was the only one with traceable ties to him who knew where he had gone when he disappeared two years ago. If Noah hadn't gone to see Peter and Martha first and cleared his head as he did, he might have said some things to Rajen he would have regretted later. As it was, Noah was more sure than ever that he was sought out and called out from that island by forces beyond either of their control: forces both heavenly and earthly. There was no way he could blame his friend for all this. By the time he arrived on campus, he could think only of giving him a big bear-hug before drilling him on any information he had about Ruth. He had now become quite focused on making things right with her—not that he didn't want to catch up with Rajen, but this would not be the first time in history when a relationship with a woman would come between two men in a friendship.

Noah wanted to avoid the Administration Office but decided that it would be the easiest way for him to find out Rajen's schedule. He was still not used to being around people, and there were certain people whom he had never quite gotten used to being around in the first place. Dr. Stuart was certainly one of those, but any familiar face would help him reenter society. Seeing Dr. Stuart actually might serve to remind Noah that most people in so-called "society" are self-serving mask-wearers and that he should remember to consider the world through that filter once again. This was actually what was flying through Noah's mind as he walked through the office door.

"Oh my God . . . Noah! How are you?" Maria nearly screamed when she saw him. She scurried around the counter to give him a hug. Noah was pleasantly surprised by the embrace. He had always liked Maria. She had a contagious, effervescent personality and the patience of Job. She needed them both on a daily basis since her job entailed standing between Dr. Stuart and the many unhappy people demanding change on campus: both faculty and students. The interns looked up as the permanent staff buzzed around Noah and pestered him with questions about where he's been and what he's been up to. He deflected the questions with the verbal judo of vagary that eventually led the conversation around to the whereabouts of Professor Golkul.

"Could you pull up Rajen's schedule for me?" he asked Maria after the awkward small talk.

"No need," she chirped. "He's in the faculty meeting. The dean has an appointment in fifteen minutes, so I can't imagine he'll keep them much longer. You can hang out here if you want."

"Thanks . . . but I think I'll take a stroll around campus. Is he still in the same office?"

"Yeah . . . we offered him yours, but he said it was too much trouble to move all his junk. I personally think he was afraid of the constant reminder of your absence."

Noah ignored the personal nature of her last comment, a practice he was now finding to be only a temporary equivocation of an unavoidable emotional encounter. Even so, he continued on as if it were never said.

"It was so nice to see you . . . I'm gonna run but I'll catch ya later." Noah took on a sudden demeanor of immediacy and dashed out the door as if running from the subject of missing old friends.

When Rajen got back to his office Noah was sitting in Rajen's chair with his feet up on the desk sipping a cup of Rajen's finest tea. Rajen was so distracted by the subject matter of the meeting he had just come from that he poured himself a cup of tea before noticing anything out of the ordinary in the small office. Just as he was turning toward the desk, Noah let fly with a hardy compliment on the quality of the tea.

"Tea's outstanding, just as I remembered it!"

Rajen jumped out of his skin and spilled tea all down the front of his white shirt. He looked up after pulling the hot shirt away from his burning skin with a look of joyful agony that briefly changed to a look of horrified guilt and then to one of pure exhilaration.

"Noah!"

He set down the cup as Noah rose from the chair and they started toward one another like two rams jousting. When they reached one another, they settled for a sort of two-handed arm wrestling handshake due to the hot liquid still scalding the surprised friend. They both broke into a fit of laughter as they couldn't coordinate the awkward arms-length embrace.

"What are you doing here?" Rajen managed to ask through the laughter.

"You tell me," Noah shot back in a pseudo-accusatory tone.

Rajen suddenly lost his smile and immediately tried to make restitution for his perceived betrayal. "I'm so sorry . . . I tried to . . . I . . . I don't know what to say."

"Relax . . . I'm just fool'n around." Noah always enjoyed getting the best of his friend, but from the look on Rajen's face, he felt maybe he should go easy on him.

"Did you get in any trouble?" Rajen asked with a more serious face than Noah had ever seen on him before.

"No, no . . . Abus is taking care of all that . . . everything's fine."

"That's a relief. You don't know how guilty I've felt since Stewart came in here with his twenty questions . . ."

"So it was Stewart . . . I knew it. That—" Noah controlled his temper.

"It felt like the inquisition. It has kept me up at night almost as much as worrying about whether you were still even alive or not," Rajen shot back in his own pseudo-accusatory tone.

"Alive and well, my friend . . . alive and well . . ." Noah trailed off and lost his smile too.

"Are you sure about that?" Rajen asked, concerned for a different reason this time. He could see that something was clearly bothering Noah.

"Yeah . . . yeah . . . I'm okay. Just trying to, you know . . . adjust to society and all."

Rajen wasn't really convinced by that answer, but he decided to let it go and change the subject. "So . . . your big adventure . . . let me hear all about it."

"Well . . . where to start? Your friend on the *Darwin's Pride* is a good man."

"Yeah. I knew I could trust him. Mostly because I know where all the bodies are buried from his unbridled college years." They both laughed in solidarity. "I still have this one picture that never made it to the network . . . that one picture alone would be enough to blackmail the devil himself."

"Well, he was more agreeable than I expected to keeping me off the books completely. Not that it did any good." Noah showed his longing to be back on the island, just for a split second, then, as always, thoughts of Ruth flooded in and caused his longing to switch loyalties.

"Again . . . I'm really sorry," Rajen said as Noah's expression reminded him of his betrayal.

"Hey, it's not your fault. You may have even done me a favor." Noah paused while working up the courage to verbalize what he hadn't been able to admit to himself yet. "I think I was running away from some unfinished business and now I have no real choice but to deal with it."

That confession was like a weight being lifted from his chest, but the reality of the conflict itself still needing to be resolved set in and it was as if someone cut the rope causing the burden to crash back onto his chest. He didn't have to get specific, Rajen knew he was talking about Ruth. The two of them sat there for a few moments playing chicken about who was going to utter her name first. Finally, Rajen could no longer take the awkward silence and the eye contact of artful avoidance. Not many could win a game of chicken with Noah McAdams. Rajen never could and today was no exception. The way things were going, it was looking as if Ruth Evans would be the first one in history to do so.

"Have you seen her or talked to her?" Rajen said with the concern of an old friend.

"Hmm?" Noah faked ignorance.

"Ruth."

"Not yet . . . I tried a couple of times, but I couldn't . . . I . . . I'm not even sure where she is. Even Peter and Martha don't know for sure. I was hoping you might know something."

"Last I knew, she was in the capital. Since your falling out, she throws Amala a message every now and then but never any real-time communication. I don't think she wants to risk having to stumble upon you in conversation. No offense," Rajen said realizing how his last statement sounded.

"The offense has been all mine . . ." Noah whispered under his breath.

"What?" Rajen asked, unsure if Noah's mumbling was in response to Rajen's verbal gaff or the subject in general.

"Nothing. You are proving to be no help at all, my friend." Noah attempted to lighten the mood.

"You expected something different? I know what I can do to help. Indian food, my place. Won't take no for an answer.

Amala and the kids would love to see you. Yes?" Rajen let the invitation hang in the air.

"Yes. Sounds great but I need to catch a transport tonight, so we'll have to make it early." Noah was just happy to be with old friends at this point. He was hoping they could help him find Ruth, but dinner with the wife and kids was enough to distract him for a few hours from his otherwise all-consuming quest.

"I have one more class, but I'll let Amala know you're coming. You can wait for me or head over there now if you'd like."

"I'll just kinda wander that direction . . . see who else I can haunt along the way." They stood and were successful at a side-to-side shoulder hug then Noah blurted, "Good luck living that one down in your next class," pointing to the large tea stain down the front of his shirt.

"Yeah, thanks a lot. Now I have to wear my lab coat. Maybe I'll make today's class a lab just to cover," Rajen said seriously. He was very aware of the students' unmerciful secret treatment of the faculty. He was reluctant to give them any unnecessary ammo. He had noticed over the years that each new generation of youth was increasingly disrespectful of their elders and very prideful. There seemed to be an underlying loathing of authority figures except when it came to the Supreme Ruler. As if magically, the generations that had grown up during his reign saw him as some sort of rock star. They even wore his image on T-shirts and hats and tote bags. It was a phenomenon difficult for many in the older generations to understand, especially since there was no respect for them whatsoever. There was something eerie about it.

Rajen grabbed his lab coat off the coat rack in the corner and headed out the door. "See ya in a bit . . . don't get lost."

"I only get lost on purpose, you know that," Noah shot back with a smile.

With Rajen gone, Noah was left alone again. It was a strange feeling. One grows accustomed to a solitary existence like one becomes numb to the cold water of the first swim of the spring. But once one has basked in the warmth of the sun amidst the numerous grains of sand on the never-ending beach, even a toe dipped back in the icy, dark vastness brings back the chilled-to-the-bone feeling that had been forgotten.

The cold feeling chased him from the office. As Noah walked down the lonely but familiar hall, he noticed the slight changes that had occurred during his absence and wondered who among the faculty was still there and who had moved on, more as a thought experiment to kill time than anything else. The distraction didn't last long and he soon found himself out in the sun with little purpose or direction.

Noah wandered aimlessly across the campus like a stray dog avoiding human contact while longing to be reunited with his pack. Eventually, he realized he was going out of his way to avoid the fountain at the center of the main quad. It flowed with too many memories and a great pain.

As was his way, he eventually faced his fear and slowly approached the center of the quad. He collapsed onto the park bench facing the fountain almost as if he were kneeling toward the icon of his lost love, searching for someone to which he could beg forgiveness.

Ruth loved this fountain, not just for its beauty but for its role as a monument to their friendship. There was a time when, almost on a daily basis, Ruth would sit there in the sun and anticipate the moment Noah would come around the corner to meet her. It was the favorite part of her day. Sometimes she would bring lunch for them, sometimes they would just lay in the grass and enjoy the sunshine, but most of the time, they would fall into deep, meaningful conversations, the type of which neither of them had ever been successful before with anyone else.

Ruth often opened her soul to him in a way she had never been capable of with anyone else and felt he was doing the same, but inevitably it would always come to a point where she felt he was shutting down or covertly putting up barriers to places in his heart and mind that even he feared to go.

The fountain was the rallying point of their friendship, a meeting place of both heart and mind, but ultimately it became ground zero for the destruction of their future together. Ruth was hopelessly in love with the man who had become her best friend and Noah was hopelessly broken and unable to admit to himself that he could love or be loved like that.

The fountain that watered their blooming relationship one day became a flood of emotional destruction. It was during what became their last, deep conversation in that place that Ruth declared her love. There is no greater destructive force than a declaration of love falling silently to the ground. Silence and peace may look similar to the outside observer, but at that moment, they could not have been more opposite. Ruth longed with everything in her for him to reciprocate, but he could not. He wanted to. He wanted to desperately, but he could not form the words.

She was devastated. She thought they had connected on a level which made this the logical next step to the relationship and, if anything, she knew him to be logical. What she didn't know was, although they shared and connected and helped one another to heal where it came to the pain of each of them losing their parents, there was another loss that he never shared with her. A lost love through a tragic death for which he blamed himself. Even now, sitting on that bench alone with his thoughts, he could not help but change the subject in his own mind and move on from that place.

As he made his way toward the main shuttle stop, he had to pass by the administration building again. It would have been quicker to cut through the building, but he told himself that since it was such a nice day outside he should take the long way around, lying to himself about his newly acquired social avoidance issues.

As he was turning onto the sidewalk that led around the building, he heard a slight tapping noise but ignored it as he continued on. Dean Stewart had been overlooking the campus from his office window as he often did and he spotted Noah lumbering toward the administration building. As Noah turned away from the entrance, the dean started tapping franticly on the window to get his attention. Not thirty seconds later, Stewart came bursting out the side entrance just as Noah came around the corner of the building.

"Dr. McAdams!" the dean blurted before Noah had a chance to look up to see who was coming out the seldom-used door. "Surely you weren't going to leave campus without saying hello, were you?"

"Oh . . . Dean Stewart . . . yeah . . . I mean no. I stopped in earlier and Maria told me you were in a meeting. How have you been?" Noah was a little flustered by being cut off at the pass by the dean, but as always, he sincerely attempted to be civil—even after finding out it was Stewart that was really responsible for giving him up. Stewart was the sort of person with whom Noah and most people, for that matter, found it easy to be angry. But Noah was starting to get over his anger about being plucked from paradise, so why stir the anger up again by taking it out on a pathetic, self-promoting weasel like Stuart? It just wasn't worth it. Forgiveness was a very important virtue to Noah. One that he knew he needed himself. An old parable of a king, a servant, and a forgiven debt flashed through his mind and his demeanor softened as they shook hands.

"Fine, just fine. So Dr. Abus found you after all . . . it's wonderful to see you again." Stewart put his other hand on top of Noah's as he shook it energetically.

Stewart was much older than Noah and had been his boss, but he had always followed him around like a puppy, as if Noah were some sort of rock star or something. It was uncomfortable for Noah, but he always tried to be nice to him. Stewart had always felt it was a great accomplishment for him to have recruited *the* Dr. Noah McAdams to the university, but what he didn't know was that Noah had really only decided to teach there to be near Peter and Martha in their retirement years. They had purchased the property nearby some years back when they discovered Martha was sick with the intention of attempting to slow down their fast-paced life. They loved South America and had spent much of their life together there, but they had some family here and they needed to be near them as well as a good medical facility at this stage in their life. Noah had followed them up from South America because he felt like family and because he needed a break from his life of roaming endlessly through the jungle. He had always planned on teaching at a university one day, so it was a fairly easy decision for him to take the position Stewart offered him. He never felt he was done making discoveries like the ones that had brought him recognition and even fame within the world of science and academia, and he certainly was not over his adrenaline junkie need for a life of adventure. But Peter and Martha were getting along in years and Martha was sick, so Noah felt it necessary to put that life on hold for a while. He would have stayed even until now if it were not for what happened with Ruth.

The conversation stalled briefly as Noah was distracted by thoughts of why he came there in the first place. Beyond that, he really didn't have much to say to the man who gave him up, forgiven or not. A stalled conversation was never a barrier to Kent Stewart, however. He simply saw it as an opportunity to talk about himself. There was no apology for giving Noah up or no real interest in where he had been and what he had been doing all this time. There was just a Kent Stewart update which entailed a long list of names dropped and a few self-aggrandizing accolades meant to cause Noah to like him more, followed by a surprising revelation.

". . . so did Professor Golkul tell you? I just told them in the faculty meeting," Stewart said toward the end of the conversation that had already gone on too long for Noah.

"Told them what?" Noah asked knowing that he was going to be sorry.

"I've just been named to the board of the Palace Council on Academic Resources. Isn't that great? Dr. Abus nominated me himself."

"Bar . . . uh, Dr. Abus did that?" Noah didn't know whether to laugh or cry. He had always underestimated Barney's knack for finding someone's weakness and exploiting it. Barney wanted to find Noah and he did whatever it took, even if it meant naming a bumbling idiot to an important position like the board of the PCAR.

"Yes, isn't that great?" Stewart repeated.

"Yeah . . . great. That's great. I'm . . . happy for you. Look, I'm really late . . ." Noah lied, "It was really nice seeing you and congratulations."

Noah headed off to the shuttle stop at top hiking pace as Stewart stood basking in the glow of thinking that he had finally impressed or even elicited jealousy from *the* Dr. Noah McAdams. Neither was true of course. Noah simply could take no more of him and had to get away to have a good laugh about the truth of how Barney had found him. He was no longer even the slightest bit angry with Rajen and was really looking forward to hearing the cries of "Uncle Noah!" while entering the house to be tackled by the children that were now most likely a foot taller than the last time he saw them. That warm thought sustained him as he rode the shuttle away from Kent Stewart and his own past at the university.

When he arrived at the house, just as he had envisioned, he was smothered by the innocence of childhood. The two children nearly knocked him over as he lowered himself to one knee to greet them. Their repetitious screams of "Uncle Noah . . . Uncle Noah!" didn't cease until he took one little head in each hand and pressed their faces into his chest. With one arm hooked under an armpit of each of the ecstatic children and while still holding their faces into his chest, he launched them into the air as he stood and spun around. Their screaming was replaced by uncontrollable laughter, muted as it was.

"My, how you've grown . . . I can barely lift you anymore!" Noah exaggerated. They were seven and nine now and certainly not too heavy for the fit adventurer to handle, but the change in them during his absence did seem too great a burden to him. He was afraid they wouldn't even remember him, but to his great delight, memories of his playful interaction were burned deep into the place in childhood that one never forgets, even when old age has stolen the present.

He soft-landed the children onto the nearby couch with much screaming, then turned into Amala's welcoming embrace. She kissed him once on each cheek with a joyful tear in her eye, then grabbed his hand to pull him into the other room where he could sit with the children while she was finishing dinner. They chatted intermittently and inanely, partially because of the playful distraction the children provided for him and partially because they both felt the need to wait for Rajen to get home before broaching any subjects of intimacy or importance. Noah didn't mind the slight awkwardness. He hated vacuous conversation, but he loved teasing the children. It was as if he were mining them for their youth, energy, and innocence and then hoarding it away in his heart for a rainy day. The smell of curry and cinnamon in the air evoked repeated compliments from Noah and helped provide a subject for small talk that lasted until Rajen arrived.

Rajen came bursting into the house just as dinner was ready to be served and was greeted by the children much the same as Noah was but in a more habitual way that didn't end in children being thrown through the air. As they sat down at the table together, the food, as good as it was, was a mere afterthought. The eating went as unnoticed as breathing as they laughed and talked with mouths full.

After catching Noah up with the news of the past two years, both global and personal— from the latest singing sensation to the children's latest school pageant and from global politics to campus politics—the family could wait no longer to hear about where Noah had been and what he had been doing. Noah told them all about his adventure of the last two years as if he were the tribe storyteller handing down oral history to the next generation. They all leaned in toward the dinner candles as if they were the flames of a flickering tribal fire, and the children listened with wide eyes and dropped jaws as he exaggerated his dangerous encounters with sharks and snakes and treacherous cliffs. They all made childish noises of disgust as he compared and contrasted Amala's curry chicken with his favorite citrus coconut rodent recipe, and all to their great amazement and in artistic detail, he concluded the adventure with a description of his homestead beside the waterfall as if it were the happily-ever-after ending to a fairy tale.

Eventually, much to the children's dismay, Noah and Rajen began to discuss the uses and benefits of the many scientific discoveries that came from his findings and experiments while he was on the island. Noah asked Rajen if he would verify some of his findings for him by running some independent controlled studies and, of course, Rajen was very honored to do so. Most of the formulae had been converted to ratios where units of measure were concerned, but before Noah left the island he placed the objects he was using as his island standards in his day pack among the few things that he brought with him. He told Rajen he would measure the objects for their equivalent mass, volume, and distance in SI units, translate the equations, and then send them to him to do the same.

Out of boredom with the professional conversation that, quite frankly, would have tortured most adults as well, little nine-year-old Riya broke in with a question, as politely as a bored nine-year-old could.

"Excuse me . . . Uncle Noah . . ." she pondered for a second while their attention turned to her, ". . . if the island was so beautiful and you loved your home there so much then . . . why did you leave? I would have stayed there forever, playing in the sand and swimming at the beach every day."

She said this with such sweet innocence that it covered gracefully over his anger with Barney for expelling him from that paradise. So much so that he could only burst into laughter with the rest of the adults as he pulled her into a bear hug to answer her question with his beard tickling her ear.

"Because I missed you so much that I just had to swim the shark-infested ocean to squeeze you and kiss your little cheeks!" he yelled into her little ear as she squirmed from the tickling of the beard, then he placed his lips on her cheek and blew air out making the silly noise of a bodily function that children love to laugh at. She squirmed even more at this as it was not only ticklish but slobbery as well.

Her little brother, Prajwat, slid off his chair, put his hands on his hips and took on an expression of angry pouting brought on by jealousy and said, "Hey . . . what about me?"

Noah looked up and took on the posture of a wildcat that has spotted its prey. "I missed you so much that the only thing I can do to stop it is to eat you alive!"

He jumped up, grabbed the boy, and put his stomach to his mouth as if he were an ear of corn. There were more squirming and silly, slobbering noises until Noah feigned exhaustion and flopped back into his chair to watch the children flee to the safety behind their mother's chair.

"Okay, children . . ." Rajen said as soon as he could quell his own laughter, "you can see that Uncle Noah is tired now. Go into the other room and play quietly as we talk some more."

The children reluctantly obeyed after several noises and gestures of protest. They kept one eye on Noah as they passed him, as if they were daring him to tickle them some more and then finally disappeared into the back room.

"She had a valid question, Noah," Amala said, thinking in the back of her mind that she knew the answer even if he didn't.

"What did Dr. Abus want?" Rajen reframed the question.

Noah knew his friends well enough to know that they were each interested in different aspects of his story. Although he didn't quite know how to tell Rajen about what Barney was asking of him, surprisingly, he was glad Rajen had limited the discussion in that way. He knew Amala's prompting was an attempt to bring the conversation around to Ruth and even though he was desperate to find out if she knew how to find her, he didn't want to actually have to talk about it.

"He . . ." Noah paused until he came to the conclusion that there was no easy way to say that they may never see him again, ". . . he offered me a position on *Epoch Utopia*."

There was silence around the table for the first time. Rajen was both excited and mournful, but he didn't know which emotion was appropriate at this point in the conversation, so he simply asked for more data like the scientist he was.

"A position? What position?" He framed the question in such a way as to be interpreted either, *What do you mean he offered you a position on a vessel that is going to leave Earth never to return?* Or, *Really? I'm happy for you. What position?*

"Director of Colonial Development," Noah stated in the same cryptic tone that Rajen was using.

There was more silence until Amala could no longer stand the emotionless chess match the two were playing. "Rajen! Just tell him!" she almost screamed in excitement.

"Tell me what?" Noah said, caught off guard by her excitement.

"I . . . well . . . we put in an application ourselves," Rajen said for the first time out loud to anyone other than his wife.

"For crew status?" Noah asked with surprise and excitement.

The couple nodded their heads with raised eyebrows and the kind of nervous smiles that are normally associated with audacious pastimes such as skydiving or bungee jumping. They all burst into laughter as they felt the relief that came from the revelation that they didn't have to go through this alone.

Rajen broke through the laughter, "It's not like we've been accepted or anything." He didn't want Noah to get his hopes up, but at the same time it was such a relief to speak of it openly and to have some hope of a continued friendship. "We haven't heard anything back at all, in fact."

That didn't matter to Noah. The mere thought of even the possibility made him excited. "Oh don't worry about that." He laughed. "What a relief! Here I was sitting here trying to figure out how I was going to explain that I may actually accept the position being forced upon me while all the time you two are trying to go of your own accord."

They all laughed some more at the irony of the situation and at their own silly fears and attempts to tiptoe around one another. The laughter and excitement so overwhelmed Amala that the filter between her brain and mouth was severed momentarily by the question that had been locked behind it since the moment Rajen called her from campus to tell her that Noah was back.

"What about Ruth?" she blurted through the laughter that then came to an abrupt end. She fought a losing battle to keep from putting her hand over her mouth as the two men stared in wide-eyed disbelief. "Oh! I'm so sorry, Noah!" she said through the fingers covering her lips.

"No . . . no . . . sorry about what?" he said with a put-on machismo that no one was comfortable with—especially Noah.

"It's just that . . . well it's hard for me not to think of her when I think of you . . . or vice versa." She continued to dig a deeper hole. "I mean I love you both so much and—"

"Forgive my wife . . ." Rajen stepped in to try and cover the offense with humor, ". . . she often drinks in the afternoon before I get home."

They all laughed again but this time uncomfortably.

"No. Really . . . it's okay," Noah said in all seriousness. "I actually am kinda relieved you brought her up. I was wondering if you might know how I can get in touch with her?"

Amala's eyes grew into those of a traditional matchmaker who had just found the perfect catch. "Really?" she chirped, with more excitement than the rocky relationship called for. "I'm so sorry though . . ." she sighed in realization, "I can only answer a direct message from her. I can't initiate one."

"Well . . . if you hear from her . . ." Noah looked down at the floor, "can you tell her that, well . . . I'm sorry and I really need to speak with her."

Noah's forlorn demeanor brought a tear to Amala's eye that she wiped on her husband's shoulder before laying her head there. "Of course, Noah," she whispered as if her words were the last dying flames of the candle of their conversation.

They all felt the finality and the couple stood up with him as he stood to leave. "I've got to catch a transport," he said before taking a cleansing breath.

Noah started for the door but was suddenly inhibited by a child clinging to each leg. They also had sensed his inevitable departure from the other room, as children are often more observant and aware than given credit for. He kissed them each on the forehead then turned silently toward the door as their parents held them each back with loving arms draped over their shoulders and across their chests.

"Keep in touch," Rajen said as the whole family followed him to the door.

"If we hear anything . . ." Amala added without finishing the statement.

The door closed behind Noah after he nodded and forced a smile in acknowledgment. The cloud over his head seemed to linger in the house for the rest of the evening, but as it is with clouds, the darkness, fear, and sadness that accompanied it eventually gave way to the hope of new life that comes from the rain left behind.

155

CHAPTER NINE

Yafeu was a peaceful man generally, but in his present state he was very capable of violence. The revelation of the cost of crew status—his own children—brought up a fury in him he had not experienced since the death of his brother. He didn't go straight home. He couldn't let his children see him like this and he certainly couldn't face his wife. After nearly getting into a bar fight just blocks away from the Space Administration complex, he spent hours wandering the travel port before he found himself on a transport to the West African coast.

The flight overshot his current home by hundreds of miles. He must have boarded it out of sheer habit or out of some deep migratory instinct. The many refugee flights of his youth often ended on the west coast very near where he was about to land. The calming blue of the Atlantic had always offered a breeze of hope for him in the past, so it felt natural for him to find himself there once again in such a time of torment.

The very reason for all of the hard work he had done to qualify for crew status was to save his children from the harsh world he had grown up in, and now he could either save some or none. It was an unacceptable choice. So many years ago, he came to the harsh conclusion that he was not capable of saving himself, much less his children, so he searched long and hard for something greater than himself to be their salvation. Others had placed the Supreme Leader in that void in their hearts and minds, but Yafeu was too smart for that. He had more faith in himself than in any other man, and if he found himself to fall short it didn't make sense for him to place another mere man in that position. Besides, he had seen charismatic leaders rise and fall over and over again, and to pledge your loyalty to one only meant violence, death, and destruction from another.

This faithlessness in men did not, however, quell his pursuit of something greater than himself. He was sure he had found it the day he first approached "the great tower in the sky." The purpose he was looking for . . . the concept being made reality right before his eyes . . . the salvation of the human race. But now, it too fell short. It fell with such a crash that Yafeu almost came undone at the core of who he was. There was nothing left but an emotional cloud of chaos where a tower of purpose once stood.

He wandered aimlessly as if covered in the chaotic dust cloud. Familiar sights, sounds, and smells eventually served to anchor him to reality, but it was as if it were the reality of the past. Something about faint memory brought on by long-forgotten surroundings was calming, but for Yafeu, such a stroll down memory lane was like a stroll through a minefield. At any moment, a sound resembling gunfire or the smell of death outside of a butcher shop could trigger the kinds of memories that he had been trying to suppress all these years, thus chasing away the fond memories of the safe haven of this coastal town as if they were refugees in his mind.

Yafeu was unsure of how he had gotten there, but as he brought his gaze up from the ground in front of him, where it had been for the last couple of hours while he had lumbered along aimlessly, he felt a sense of home. It was strange really, since this was never home for him, but the dilapidated little structure on the edge of the dunes still stood. It stood for safety in his mind and caring in his heart as surely as the cross on the roof still stood. It was riddled with bullet holes and there was evidence of fire, but it stood through it all.

Yafeu peeked through the open window next to the main door and, after finding it empty, he gingerly pushed the door open with a creak.

"Hello?" he almost whispered. His greeting was swallowed up by the single room full of hard, wooden benches. It rattled around the rafters holding the tin roof for a few seconds then faded into memory as if to take the place of all the memories of this place flooding to the surface.

It was strange to find the place empty. He had always remembered it teeming with people in need helping those in greater need. It was the one place that he felt cared for by being empowered to care for others. Oddly, the emptiness seemed to show solidarity with his mood, so he made his way to the front and let his on-call bag fall to the floor in front of the cross as if he were laying a burden there. The inviting sound of the weight hitting the floor caused his knees to buckle with great faith in the wooden bench beneath his muscular frame, and as it caught him, the tears of many years came flowing. He placed his elbows on his knees and buried his face in his hands to try to hide from his own foolishness and shame. He hadn't cried since he mourned his brother and had promised himself that there would be nothing else worthy of his tears. Again, he could not even live up to his own standards. He failed his brother, he failed his wife, he failed his children . . . he failed himself . . . he failed the Project. The one thing greater than himself he found worthy of placing his faith in had turned right around and told him he was not worthy of it. As Yafeu stood outside of himself, he witnessed his own undoing. It was brutal and sad and hopeless.

He had never felt hopeless before, strangely enough. Even after all the death and destruction he had witnessed and fled from in his youth. He was starting to realize that the reason he found himself back at this little mission was because this was the place that had infused him with hope as a child. He saw with his own eyes people raising themselves out of the depths of despair by some miraculous invisible power. He never understood that power, but he was infused with hope nonetheless. He remembered stories of a loving God and of a Son and a cross, but it was all very confusing to him as a child since he had never seen love that didn't end in death. This story, for many, did seem to end in the death of a Son; but at the same time, he saw a living hope in some of those people, the ones who told him that the story didn't end there, that the death of the Son was only the beginning, that He wasn't still dead. That always confused Yafeu, *What did they mean, not still dead?* As if death wasn't permanent. He had seen enough death in his unfortunate youth to know that one does not recover from it.

Of course, he was familiar, even as a child, with beliefs about an afterlife and the worship of ancestors who were long departed from this world, but to him that was just what it said, an afterlife. Those who had come before us had moved on to something else: to death, something less real somehow, the abode of the spirits. To say that someone is not still dead is to fly in the face of his understanding of the world. It either mocked the death of all those he loved or proclaimed hope.

Yafeu had seen the powerful effects this dichotomy had on people, no matter which way they saw it. Those who saw it as mocking were moved to yet more violence and those who saw it as hope were empowered to withstand any persecution. He was always afraid he would end up like the former; that the violence poured into him as a child would inevitably cause him to grow into a man just as violent. A man who saw every attempt by well-meaning people to reach out to him with optimism and a message of hope for the future as mockery of his pain which must be met with violence. That was his fear, not his hope. His hope was that he also could find the power within to withstand any trial and, like the people he met in this place long ago, still have the ability to love and act humanely. The people in this place had infused him with enough hope to be capable of great love for his wife and children, but powerful love comes with powerful consequences. He saw this new revelation about the reality of crew status as both an attack on who he was at his very core and an attack on his family. He so wanted to act out violently, but there was no amount of violence that could change the situation. He could not kill, steal, and destroy his family's way onto *Epoch Utopia*. He could only surrender to reality.

Afzal Jamail Sargon, however, would never surrender. He did kill, steal, and destroy his way onto *Epoch Utopia*. With himself at the center of his own universe, the end justified the means. The end . . . being at the center of everyone else's universe. The means . . . human sacrifice. Not a blood-stained altar, a dripping dagger and a recently beating heart held high above the head; he was too cunning to be so conspicuously evil. Nevertheless, the blood flowed red and thick and cried out loudly from the ground beneath his feet. As Sargon conquered, there was unmerciful slaughter in region after region until everyone watching said to themselves, *Who can stand against him?* There were those who fell victim to the death traps of his overreaching demands. The Mars colony served now as nothing but their tombstone, a barren monument to his hubris. And then there were those in his inner circle, those who served as examples of the cost of betrayal or simple ineptitude. It was this last group that resembled most closely the dripping dagger and bloody heart held up for all to see. The general public was never to see Sargon as anything but a benevolent father, ushering humanity into a glorious future, but for that to happen, those responsible for that image had to see him as an unmerciful enforcer, calmly wiping the blood of their colleagues off his hands.

There was no turning him back. Afzal Jamail Sargon was going to sail off into space, history, and mythology—no matter how many souls had to be sacrificed along the way. The destruction of the Mars colony had little to no bearing on his course. In fact, it almost seemed to strengthen his resolve. *Epoch Utopia* was now the vehicle of his spite toward whatever higher power responsible.

Although spite seemed to be the first reaction Yafeu had toward those responsible for the desolation of his dream, there really was no spite in him. He was undone—at the bottom with nowhere to look but up. He was willing to turn but he felt he had nowhere to turn. It took an unseen power working in his unconscious self to return him to a place where he could see hope. This hope he had once seen from afar, now seemed strangely close, as if hope lives at the bottom where there is no place to look but up. Look up he did and soon found himself pleading, even praying, for this hope to be within his grasp so he could consume it and integrate into his very soul.

CHAPTER TEN

The flight back to the capital would have seemed uneventful to anyone traveling with Noah if, in fact, he didn't tend to travel alone. But behind his deceptively calm eyes, there was a tempest blowing. He could not get away from thoughts of Ruth, yet, just as in his dreams, she was still beyond his grasp. To make it all worse, these were not just random thoughts as one may have of an old friend, or girlfriend in this case, when reminded of them by a fragrance or a déjà vu circumstance. These were real laments of love lost, torturously and inseparably married to a knowledge of a greater calling and purpose for the yet unrealized relationship. It was more than he could take. He was more certain than ever that he was supposed to step off this planet in faith to be a light for those floating in the darkness of space and that Ruth was an undeniable and indispensible brushstroke in this, what was going to have to be a masterpiece of faith. But that was his problem—faith . . . faith and hope. He found himself despairing. It was, of course, unlike him to do so normally, but when it came to matters of the heart, he had more than one deep-seated issue of pain and loss that hindered faith. It was the protection of this very pain that caused him to hurt her in the first place, and now he was finding that defense mechanisms inevitably cause more pain than they numb and for more people than just oneself. He was finding himself without hope of finding Ruth before departure and without faith that she would forgive him if he did.

Realizing he was despairing and that he was not finding any solace at the bottom of his glass of scotch, he set it down on the tray of the serving-bot as it passed him making its rounds through the aisles of the aircraft. He, instead, looked for some in the box under his seat. He had carried on the box that Peter had given him and, with no little effort, he had been able to force it into the void beneath him. The struggle to wrestle it from its hiding place elicited annoyed looks from the other passengers that were elevated to gasps of disgust when, after setting it on the seat next to him, he opened the cover to reveal that the whole commotion was over nothing but worthless old books. The furrowed brows asked the question, *Haven't you ever heard of an electronic pad?* Noah ignored their ignorance as he thumbed through some of the delicate pages and they eventually traded the distraction he had provided for whatever distractions they were previously enslaved by.

As he looked over the treasure trove, Noah felt so grateful to Peter for the priceless gift. Barring the Ruth situation, leaving Peter and Martha behind was going to be the most difficult thing for him. These few personal items and more importantly what they stood for, along with Peter's own writings, made it seem as if somehow, some small part of them was coming with him. In reality it was no small part. Peter and Martha had downloaded so much of themselves into Noah's heart over the years that even after their passing, much less the separation of the emptiness of space, they would live on through Noah, and possibly his children, in this reality as surely as they would live on in eternity. This thought helped him to float down gracefully from the storm of despair in his head just as the aircraft began to float down toward Two Rivers Travel Port.

His next meeting with Dr. Abus was not scheduled until the next day, but since he would have to pass Barney's office in the Palace complex to get to his new apartment, also within the walls of the complex, he thought he would stop in and say hello and maybe see if there were any more briefing materials he needed to look over before their official meeting. It was unsettling to him that all the security agents knew exactly who he was, called him by name, and ushered him straight through the checkpoints. Strangely, he would have felt more at ease if they would have scrutinized him and questioned him and asked him what his business there was.

Noah preferred anonymity, which was antithetical to the culture he was now being forced to be a part of. Most people, like Kent Stuart, were striving for whatever measure of fame or notoriety they could gluttonously gather to themselves. Even after achieving some very notable things very early in his career, Noah turned down book deals and interviews and speaking engagements and all the pop culture talk show appearances. To him it was the achievement itself and how it could benefit mankind that mattered, not notoriety and a shallow fifteen minutes of fame. This attitude resulted in great fame among the scientific and academic communities but little to no recognition by the general public, which was perfectly fine with him. There was the odd news story now and then, done without his cooperation, that mentioned his name when dealing with the subjects to which he had made major contributions, but they were few and far between.

Although he preferred anonymity, this was not really the source of his concern regarding the security force. He knew that Dr. Abus had given him clearance to get in and out of the complex and all, but there was something eerie about the whole situation. Everyone he had dealt with among Abus's staff and Palace security seemed to know specific details about him that should not be available to them. He had prided himself for years on being able to effectively stay off the grid. He suspected long ago that network searches and possibly even conversations and even people's locations were being monitored and even manipulated. He didn't get an implant and he very rarely used his earpiece for this very reason and to the great frustration of everyone he knew or worked with. Even most of his net research was done through pseudonyms or even students and lab assistants. He had gone through so much trouble to keep the dying spirit of individual liberty and privacy alive, seemingly to no avail. It seemed to him that some of the things waiting for him in his apartment, like the scotch, the Swiss chocolate, and Ethiopian coffee, could only have come from someone who knew him. If it were not for the fact that he didn't think Barney had the memory or the forethought for such things, he would have felt honored. As it was, he felt spied upon and violated.

He left the security checkpoint behind and shook off the urge to look over his shoulder as he turned the corner into the cabinet office complex. He did his best to put thoughts of some evil grand conspiracy behind as he walked up the steps into the building. This proved to be quite difficult since he couldn't help but take in his surroundings. The very buildings themselves exuded sheer political power through an opulence that was meant to be intimidating. Noah wasn't at all intimidated, but he was humbled by it all. Not by the marble and the gold and the architecture or seemingly impossible feats of engineering but by his, rather unwilling, place amidst it all. It seemed as if he were being carried along by a powerful current flowing straight toward his place in the world—the world? No, it was now bigger than that even. He was very familiar with this particular flow and its source. It was not the same current that most others were riding. In fact, it was diametrically opposed—anti-parallel, if you will. It was like where the mighty Amazon meets the ocean. At certain places, it could seem as if the river was flowing upstream. Though the flow he was in was less crowded, it was not without obstacle and even opposition. At times it felt as if he were about to be dashed against jagged rocks only to find that the flow carried him swiftly and harmlessly by. Other times he would decide to swim against its power, to a place of comfort he had already passed, which only resulted in struggle to the point of fatigue. With the help of Peter and Martha, he learned to prostrate himself within the flow and rest in its power—to trust it no matter how good or bad the surroundings seemed. Until this point, he merely had to trust that the flow was carrying him to his place in the grand scheme of things, but now he was actually beginning to catch a glimpse of that destination and it did not seem to be at all what he had envisioned. On top of that, he was leaving behind his swimming instructors and his partner was nowhere to be found. As he thought about the power of the current and the purposefulness of its ebb and flow, he had a moment of inspiration which sparked a germ of faith that his partner was not far away, perhaps just on the other side of a surrounding crest.

As Noah was approaching Dr. Abus's suite lost in thought, Lisa, who had also been lost in thought, glanced up at the hall-cam window in the corner of her view screen to see him reaching for the door handle of the reception office. She stood abruptly and walked toward the back hallway while motioning to the nearest aide.

"Go tell Dr. Abus that Dr. McAdams is here," she ordered in an intentional monotone.

"Yes, ma'am."

The aide ran off in the opposite direction, but did not find the doctor at his desk where he would normally be at this time of day. Dr. Abus had stepped outside for a moment to stretch his legs. As he came in the back entrance, he caught a glimpse of Lisa at the other end of the hall making a quick U-turn as if she had forgotten something important in the back office. He thought nothing of it and continued into the main office area. As he rounded the corner, he met the aide who then informed him of their unexpected guest, who was himself coming into the main area from the front entrance.

"Dr. McAdams . . ." Abus said with delight and false formality, "we weren't expecting you until tomorrow."

"Well, I figured I better show up on my own terms this time before you come looking for me with an armed assault team again."

They both laughed in a way that was unsettling to the surrounding staff. They had never seen anyone interact with the Minister in such a way. The awkwardness for the staff continued as the two old friends shot friendly insults back and forth as if they were two mates down at the pub trying to get the best of one another for the amusement of the crowd. Any laughter among this crowd, however, was kept inside. Apart from a few camouflaged smiles and eye-catching glances among the staff members, they continued on with the utmost of professional behavior.

After circling around for several minutes, they finally landed upon the subject of Noah's visit and both thought that they should continue their conversation in Barney's office. As they turned to head that way, Barney stopped abruptly and turned back around as if looking for someone.

"Have you met my Chief of Staff yet?" Dr. Abus asked as he scanned the room for her.

"No, I don't think so," Noah answered.

"Go get Lisa, she's in the back," Dr. Abus ordered the very same aide that had been tasked by Lisa to come find him.

He scurried off into the back hall and after a short time he reappeared ahead of the sound of some very intentional footsteps. As Lisa came around the corner, Noah looked up and gasped audibly.

"Ruth!?" he blurted uncontrollably.

"Hello, Noah," she said with a softness that defied her stern posture. Even as she said it, her countenance changed. She said it matter-of-factly but with an undertone of intimacy that betrayed her attempts to hide her history with Noah from Abus and the rest of the staff.

"Ruth?" Dr. Abus said in confusion before he put all the pieces together in his head. "Ahh . . . yes . . . Ruth." He nodded as he gazed off into the space of his distant memories.

The first day she came on board as part of Abus's staff, years ago, before she showed herself so competent as to become his Chief of Staff, he interviewed her briefly and saw in her file that her first name was Ruth but that she went by Lisa for reasons unimportant to him. It was a short interview because she had a letter of recommendation from Dr. Noah McAdams who was listed as one of her professors. Both of these details, her real name and her connection to Noah, were quickly forgotten by the old man until this moment. Years of everyone calling her Lisa and of her giving no hint of familiarity with Noah any time he broke into one of his nostalgic musings about the good ol' days when *the* Dr. Noah McAdams led him through the jungle and saved his life, had served to erase any connection in his mind between Noah and Lisa.

Noah stood frozen and speechless. It took every ounce of strength within him not to run to her, sweep her up into his arms, and plant his most passionate kiss on her, but he didn't yet know if he was even welcome in her presence, much less with what his gesture of passion would be returned—open arms and a kiss as passionate, or a kick in the groin. He was willing to chance the kick in the groin, but even at the height of the passion of the moment he was unwilling to dishonor her in front of her colleagues with such a physical display.

He was, after a long awkward pause, able to break the silence with an opening, heartfelt gesture, "Ruth . . . I'm so glad to see you . . . I've been looking all over for you."

She stared back at him in an emotionless manner that almost concealed what she was thinking. *Oh yeah . . . since when, jackass?*

Lisa had manipulated Noah to the top of Abus's list of potential candidates because she was torn between wanting Noah to sail away into space, thus being out of even the possibility of being in her life, and her hopeless desire to see him again for any reason at all. She told herself that if he was chosen, maybe then she could finally put him behind her and get on with life. She had been attempting to hide the pain of losing Noah by immersing herself in her work, just as she had attempted to hide the pain of losing her parents by immersing herself in her studies. Like before, her affinity toward immersion "therapy" distracted her for awhile but proved to be ultimately unsuccessful the day she saw Noah's name on Abus's info request list. After the first crying session came the anger, and then after that came the dream of being reunited happily ever after but, ultimately, her fear of further rejection won out and she foolishly planned to always be elsewhere when Noah was around Abus, for the short period of time remaining before departure.

She should have known this was going to be an impossible task, but she stubbornly put the plan into motion and adjusted it along the way, as needed, until, that is, Noah showed up unannounced and, typically, not according to her carefully constructed schedule. She had found herself trapped in the back office with no way to escape. The worst thing was, she knew that Abus knew she was in there and it would be mere moments before he would call her out to meet his old friend that he had told her so much about. She couldn't escape out the back entrance because she would have to walk right past the main office area where she could hear them laughing and talking. She had been cowering in the corner behind a cabinet when the aide came in to relay the message. He found her white as a ghost with head bowed and a hand over her mouth and nose, hugging herself with the other. She was staring at the floor in either unbreakable concentration or borderline mental and emotional breakdown—he didn't know which. As he addressed her respectfully, she had no choice but to sheepishly move toward the emotional slaughter that was sure to take place. As she came to the door to the main office area, she threw her head up, arched her back, squared her shoulders, and marched into the room with the air of confidence that everyone in the office was so familiar with. Only the aide had seen the brief glimpse of the real woman always hiding inside her.

Before she could respond, Noah continued his plea for mercy, "I went to see Peter and Martha, thinking they would know where to find you, but . . . you know . . . they miss you very much . . ." When he said that, Lisa suddenly became Ruth again and the stern, emotionless expression softened but just for a moment. The moment was not long enough for Noah, or anyone else in the room for that matter, to tell if they were about to witness laughter or tears. The emotionless mask returned, but this time everyone could see that it was, indeed, a mask.

Abus could see, uncharacteristically, that everyone in the room was uncomfortable with the conversation. "Perhaps you two should finish this conversation in my office."

If the staff was uncomfortable with the previous jocular exchange between the two doctors, they really were now, yet they found themselves, this time, unable to mask their reactions. They were uncomfortable, yes, but hopelessly drawn into the soap opera unfolding before them.

Ruth turned and started walking briskly toward the back hall, away from Abus's office.

Noah stood frozen until Barney shoved him that direction. "You'd better go after her, my man."

She turned back briefly as if she were going to say something, saw the whole room staring at her, and then spun back and continued on, which again froze Noah in his tracks. She took a few more steps and turned impatiently, raised her eyebrows, tightened her lips around clenched teeth, and motioned with her head toward the back door while cryptically yet cartoonishly waving him over with a quick motioning of the hand that almost comically effected no movement in her stiff body except from the elbow down.

Noah had seen that expression before and knew he had better find some motion in his legs somehow. Noah never scurried, but if he were to, it would look much like what he was doing now to catch up to Ruth as she clacked through the hall in her expensive, high heels toward the back door. As soon as they both cleared the door and it slid shut behind them, she turned and faced him with her hands on her hips. She stopped so suddenly that he nearly ran into her. He apologized softly with his body language and then he too regained his composure with a posture that was not unaffected by hers.

The staff gathered around the nearest windows to watch the drama unfold, hiding behind the self-tinting glass energized by the desert sun. There were whispers and nervous giggles as they watched. None of them had imagined that the "Ice Queen," who had surpassed them all to become their boss, had a history, especially not one so juicy with a famous humanitarian who was looking hot and lean with his tropical tan and bad-boy, carefree attitude. The women made crude comments the likes of which, in days past, would only have fouled the mouths of sailors and construction workers. The men played it cool, as if the comments didn't make them jealous which, of course, they did; particularly the ones who had been trying to evoke this very response from the women since they started working together.

There was a momentary silence as the two stared one another down until Ruth broke it harshly with a sarcastic tone of self-preservation, "Well?"

Noah knew he probably deserved what was coming to him, but he found himself lashing out defensively nonetheless, "What do you mean, *well?* You were here this whole time and you let me go halfway around the world looking for you?"

"How was I to know you were looking for me? You never once gave me any reason to believe you ever had any intention of coming to find me before!"

Noah softened a little, knowing he was guilty as charged. "I'm sorry . . . I mean . . . really . . . I'm really sorry. I've been needing to say that to you for a long time now."

She turned her back and crossed her arms. As she was war-gaming responses in her head, she nervously balanced one foot on the heel of her shoe while playing with the heel strap with the toe of her other foot. Not finding a response that satisfied her, she spun back around and impatiently blurted, "Can we talk about this later? I have a lot—"

"No!" Noah said resolutely, "I've put this off for far too long. I let you go with . . . with things unsaid before and it was the biggest mistake of my life! I'm not going to do it again." His tone was stern but in a passionate way. His demeanor revealed his self-torture. Anyone else watching could have mistaken it for anger with her, but she knew him too well. He was seldom angry with others, especially her. He was angry with himself for letting it . . . for letting them get to this point.

Part of her wanted to soothe him and take his pain away, but then again, there was the more prominent part of her that was very hurt by the way they parted, and misery loves company. She found herself giving him more and more rope so that she could ride in and save him just before he was about to hang himself with it. This desire to see him squirm was unlike the Ruth he knew all those years ago, but the innocent girl he had let walk out of his life was now a seasoned political operative—hardened by the relational survival tactics of the very capital of the world.

As the conversation regressed from a simple apology to the dredging up of things thought to have been long forgotten, Noah noticed she was becoming more and more cryptic in her comments and that she moved freely between open and closed postures, depending on the subject at hand. After a while he came to a realization. "Don't act like you don't care . . . it was you . . . it was all you!"

"What are you talking about?" she said as she broke eye contact while still doing her best to look innocent.

He took her hand, touching her for the first time since before they went their separate ways. "The scotch, the Swiss chocolate, the coffee, even the very décor of the apartment. That was all you. Don't tell me there wasn't a little tender love and care there."

"Yeah, well . . . don't read anything into it," she said as she slowly and reluctantly removed her hand from his.

As she tried to turn toward the door, he gently turned her face back toward him with a meek hand, commanding direct eye contact one last time. "I really am sorry . . . I don't want things to end this way . . . or at all. Please, if you can find it in your heart . . . forgive me?"

She looked into his eyes for longer than she intended to, then she returned to herself and turned toward the door. "I've got a lot of work to do."

As she rushed back in the door, staff members could be seen scurrying in every direction like a herd of antelope, surprised by a cheetah. She was so conflicted that she didn't even notice them. She only made it a few steps into the building before she stopped herself dead in her tracks, spun around in a fury, and charged at him.

"No . . . you know what . . ." she said in the manner she had always fantasized she would if she ever had the chance and the courage, "I told you that I love you and you just let me stand there . . ." She put her hand up to keep him from interrupting. "I told you that I was leaving and you just let me go . . . with barely a goodbye."

Noah gave her a moment before he attempted an explanation. "I know this may sound . . . well . . . I didn't . . . I didn't want to stand in the way of you becoming . . . who you were meant to be."

Ruth tried to stay mad at him. "Did it ever occur to you that, just maybe, I was meant to be with you?"

"Well, it has now . . ." he said in a manner that reflected the angry playfulness he was sensing from her.

"You never came after me . . . never so much as called!" Her eyes welled up, but she forced herself back to anger.

"This is me . . . coming after you," Noah said with a little too much energy, then his voice softened, "Is it . . . I don't know . . . too little, too late?"

Having sufficiently vented, Ruth let out a deep breath and returned to the unreadable political operative she had become. "You're kinda slow for a genius, aren't ya?" She turned and calmly returned to the office—for good this time.

Noah stood, staring at her perfect form walking away from him until the door slid between them. "What does that mean?" he muttered under his breath. Since he couldn't answer that question, he felt it best to give her some space. He didn't return through the building. If Barney needed him, he knew where to find him. As Noah escaped out the back gate, he walked by the landing pad occupied by the aircraft that had caused such turbulence and turmoil on his beach only days ago. It seemed like years ago to him now because of his all-encompassing quest to find Ruth. He had convinced himself that finding her would bring peace to his tortured soul, but the tempest inside was blowing stronger than ever. As an adventurer and adrenaline junkie, he had always thrived on that sick feeling in the pit of the stomach, but this was more than he could stand. To turn back toward the face of someone you love and ask forgiveness, that was hard enough, but to be denied forgiveness was unbearable; for to be denied forgiveness on one's own terms is the very definition of hell. Grace . . . mercy . . . that was all he could hope for now. He could never return the lost years he stole from her . . . from himself . . . from them, with his stubborn unwillingness to expose the pain he carried in his heart. It was no gentle irony that it was the fear of losing her that kept him from allowing himself to have her, and now it seemed as if he was going to lose her twice.

The once energetic and athletic adventurer now found that his knees could barely carry him the few hundred meters back to his apartment. He fumbled his way through his door and managed to get to the couch before collapsing. With his face pressed heavily against the seat cushion, he stared for hours at the bottle of scotch on the coffee table. Fond memories turned to regrets. Anger, sadness, and happiness lost all borders within him. He had not prepared himself for the possibility that his quest would end this way. He even felt betrayed by his very dreams and was now more confused than ever about his purpose and calling. He had been prepared to tell Dr. Abus he would accept the position, but now his whole life seemed to be up in the air. He knew of the dangers of finding purpose and worth in anyone other than the Creator, but he was genuinely confused because he thought that it was being made clear to him that Ruth was part of his newfound calling. Maybe he was simply supposed to ask her for forgiveness before he departs and that was all that there was to that? Not that forgiveness is a small thing, offering it or receiving it, but the dreams seemed to be quite a dramatic extreme to be used to get that point across. Maybe it was all out of a guilty conscience. If indigestion can cause nightmares, certainly a little old-fashioned guilt could cause reoccurring dreams. His faith waned for a while down such side streets in his mind. After a few more hours, his faith seemed to revert to the size of a mustard seed. He determined to fulfill his calling, with or without Ruth, and uttered the solemn phrase, "Thy will be done" softly and repeatedly.

As he was about to doze off, he was unsure but he thought he heard the doorbell ring. He didn't get up, thinking that it was Barney and knowing that if he wanted in, he would come in. It rang a second time and then was followed by a light tapping. He peeled himself off the couch and lumbered to the door. He was still half asleep when he slowly opened it and then stood wide eyed and dumbfounded.

"You're kinda slow for a genius, aren't ya?"

Ruth threw her arms around his neck and kissed him with the same passion he felt the moment he saw her in the office.

After the long, passionate kiss, Noah was barely able to keep himself together, but he managed to take her face in his hands to lock eyes with her. From a place deeper in his heart than he was ever willing to go before came the words she had been waiting years to hear, "I love you."

As he confessed his love, Ruth's cheeks blushed the bright red he remembered from the first day he met her. In his mind, he was back taking attendance in the first class of the morning, all those years ago.

"Ruth Evans," Dr. McAdams called as he continued down the attendance list.

"Most people call me Lisa," a timid voice said from the front row but furthest from the lectern.

"It says here, *Ruth Elisa*?" Noah questioned in an unusual moment of personal interaction with a student.

"Just Lisa," she replied. "Only my family calls me Ruth . . ." *but you can call me Ruth any time,* she thought as her heart started to race, adding a little extra pink to her cheeks.

"How 'bout I just call you, *Miss Evans*?" Noah said, more for his own benefit as he found her blushing to be adorable. He knew from that moment on, she was going to be a distraction.

Noah never did call her Lisa. He continued to call her Miss Evans until her time under his tutelage was up. He also avoided her as much as possible in the halls, or wherever, so he likely never even heard her friends call her Lisa. It was a long semester for him because he avoided visiting Peter and Martha as well, since she was staying with them. He didn't want to make it too obvious, so he did drop by every now and then when he knew she would be at another class or out with friends, but he did not make it to one Sunday dinner at the Abramses that whole semester.

Other professors *fraternized* with their students all the time. It was, of course, frowned upon by the university, officially, but hedonistic as the world was, it was unofficially seen as unavoidable and, let's face it . . . a whole lot of fun. Noah was different in that he had a very high moral standard personally. He was also different from just about all of the other professors in that he was nearly the same age as most of the students when he started teaching there. The other faculty could not understand his reluctance. Considering the way some of the girls threw themselves at them, a handsome young man like him could choose from the cream of the crop as far as they were concerned. It wouldn't even seem creepy to others the way it often did for most of them. Even so, Noah remained resolute. This time, it was not easy. Ruth did not "throw herself" at him in the way the other girls did. That was the problem. Immodesty and innuendo were a put-off to Noah; it was easy to ignore those girls. Ruth, however, had a purity and innocence about her that was very attractive to Noah. Little did Noah know that it was an outward innocence but innocence all the same; she was not innocent of trying to place herself within his path. She knew his daily schedule the same as he knew hers. He looked hers up in an effort to stay out of her way, but she acquired his through careful attentiveness that bordered on stalking. Let's just say that she went a little out of her way between classes, just a little bit, every day, until she had his routine mapped out as if she were a naturalist studying a new species. She would even linger at a particular table in the student center, pretending to read or work until she saw him come out of the faculty lounge. As soon as she saw him, she would look up at the clock, surprised, throw her e-pad into her bag, and scurry off in front of him—pretending all along that she had no idea he was there. This on the day when he had to walk all the way across campus, she didn't even have a class over there at that time.

Needless to say, Noah went right from calling her Miss Evans to calling her Ruth the very first Sunday dinner after the semester ended. Sunday dinners turned to weeknight dinners more often than not and that turned to midnight snacks—you know . . . to help her study. Noah tried to stay away from her until she finished her masters and was no longer a student at the university, but he just couldn't. It was bad enough waiting until she was no longer *his* student. They both used the excuse that her degree program was political science and she only needed the one physical science class. She would not be taking any more of the classes that he taught. The excuse was for Noah only, no one else even cared—not even Peter and Martha. They were thrilled. They had never seen either one of them so happy.

It was not an affair; it was a friendship, a deep and genuine friendship. Not that there wasn't chemistry and desire, there was, but it was not the same animal that most experienced. This was not the temporary, *get what you can out of it fling* that people their age use up and throw away; this was *I care about you and what is best for you, whether or not it involves me.* The people around them did not recognize it, except for Peter and Martha; they knew it all too well. Most people thought it strange that they spent so much time together yet they did not seem to be *together* in the sense that they understood.

All of that was ancient history. Noah and Ruth now had a chance to write a future for themselves if they could only wipe the slate clean and start over. After declaring his love, Noah led her inside as if they were dancing and the two of them, together, commenced the long, arduous task of cleaning the slate.

It was a very long night filled with the paradox of pleasure and pain. They had both missed the other so intensely that simply being in one another's presence brought such joy and excitement, that it was hard to concentrate on the real work that had to be done. The work of digging out the emotional splinters of a shipwrecked relationship and the even harder work of clearing away the obstacles beneath the surface that caused the wreck in the first place.

Noah, for the first time, told Ruth the painful story of his first love. How they grew up together. How she helped him through the death of his parents. How she got sick and how he blamed himself for her death, having found a cure, only too late to save her. He couldn't bring himself to go into any real detail or even utter her name, but Ruth was finally able to understand or at least recognize that Noah had a serious, even clinical, cause underlying his commitment issues. Everyone he had ever loved had left him tragically. *Of course* he had to battle his subconscious self-protection reflex. If she had ever been able to think logically concerning him, she would have realized this long ago.

They both realized that commitment issues were now obsolete neuroses. They could not possibly exist within a being who has contemplated and ultimately accepted a call to leave Earth forever with a small band of the fellow committed. There was no time left to be hindered by such things. The mission was upon them.

After hours of peaks and valleys traversed together, the conversation finally came around to the subject of whether or not Noah was going to accept the position. Neither one of them wanted to speak first on the matter for fear of the other's unknown response. They both knew that, if he accepted, the impending deadline would force them to the immediate decision point of committing to one another, once and for all, or saying goodbye forever. After the long night of healing, they both knew they did not want to say goodbye forever.

The dilemma causing the silence on the subject centered around Noah's ignorance of whether Ruth would even consider being a part of such an insane mission that calls for leaving behind everything one has ever known and everyone one has ever loved. What he should have known, long ago, is that, besides Peter and Martha, he was the only one she loved.

For Ruth, silence on the subject came from her newly discovered insight into his tendency to run when faced with real commitment. After their long night together, she was now sure that she wanted to be wherever he was, regardless of the consequences, but she did not want to spook him by speaking first on the subject.

Noah finally broke the silence.

"I am not losing you again . . ."

Noah paused as he realized that what he was going to say after that would have shifted the heavy burden of the decision to join the mission onto her and that's the last thing he wanted. He was going to say *Wherever you go, I go*, but instead he ordered firmly, "You're coming with me!"

At that moment, whatever remnant of the façade of prideful self-reliance that was left to her demeanor fell away as she buried her cheek in his chest and said, "Wherever you go, I go."

"Well . . ." Noah said with a sigh, "I guess we're going on a little trip then."

They embraced silently for a long time. Each allowing the other's presence to soothe the raging storm of doubt and worry within them. After a time, they both felt as if they could conquer anything, as long as they were together.

"So, I just have one more thing to ask you," Noah whispered in her ear as he reached up to the shelf behind her head and pulled down the picture frame he had rescued from exile at Peter and Martha's.

Ruth had been so focused on overcoming the conflict of the night, she hadn't noticed it until that moment. She was starting to feel overcome with emotion again as she saw it, but she kept strong, until he broke a piece off the back.

"What are you doing?" she gasped, as the photo was one of her most prized possessions.

He smiled playfully then dropped to one knee while revealing the broken piece as the treasure it was. He had removed one of the hanging rings from the back of the frame and was now slipping it onto her finger.

"Ruth Elisa Evans . . . will you marry me?"

Having already worked out their fears and future over the long night, she returned his playful obviousness with a tearful, "It's about time, ya big jerk!"

"Come on now . . . I have to hear the word," he said, almost desperately.

She lifted him up to her face and with all seriousness looked into his eyes and spoke life, "Yes!"

If anyone else had been there to witness the scene, it would have seemed comical and possibly corny, but to them it was a welcome return to the youthful joy that only rears its head in private moments between soulmates.

They collapsed together onto the couch and almost immediately fell to sleep. Each feeling more peaceful than they had ever felt before.

When morning came, Dr. Abus stopped off at Noah's apartment on his way to the office. He was still unsure of Noah's level of commitment to the grand mission that had been lain before him, and they were running out of time before the next press conference. Abus knew Noah may still need some convincing and he thought the privacy and comfortable surroundings of Noah's apartment would serve his purpose best.

As before, Abus let himself in and in a rare moment of embarrassment, for all involved, Abus took two steps in, then spun around and headed back out in the same dance-like manner that had come over him when Noah let the rodents out of their cages back on the island. When Abus had walked in, the first thing he saw was Noah spooning on the couch with none other than his very own Chief of Staff. The noise of the door opening roused the two just in time for them to see him peek back behind the closing door. They both shot to their feet and straightened their clothing, then Noah jogged to the door to catch him before he left.

There was really nothing to be embarrassed about. They were both fully clothed and had only fallen asleep in each other's arms after staying up all night talking. They had a lot to say to one another and the emotional conversation was as physically taxing on them as any other activities Barney may have mistook them to be engaged in, so Noah could see how he may have gotten the wrong impression.

Ruth was embarrassed for the simple reason that she allowed her boss to see her as anything other than a superhuman, no-nonsense, miracle worker. She was upset with herself that she had lost track of time and was now going to be late to the office. In reality, there was no such thing as *late* to the office for her. She had no official office hours. She was the boss to everyone but Dr. Abus. She had always made a point of being there before he got there and staying until after he left, and now her perfect streak was broken—not to mention she let him see her as an emotional being with romantic interests.

Noah called out the door meekly for Dr. Abus to return and as Ruth heard his voice, all of her initial thoughts of embarrassment and frustration took a back seat to her memories of the healing hours of reconciliation they shared overnight. She walked to the door, kissed Noah on the cheek, and put her head down while fighting the urge to put her hand over her face as she passed Dr. Abus on her way out. They both mumbled, "morning" awkwardly and simultaneously while avoiding eye contact.

Abus reentered the apartment and closed the door behind him. At that moment, the esteemed cabinet minister disappeared and Noah's old friend Barney stood there staring with a mischievous smile.

"Good for you, ol' chap!" Barney let fly, playfully.

Noah was speechless. He actually still couldn't believe it himself. It was all happening so fast.

"So, I take it she forgave you?" Barney said, breaking the awkward silence.

"It was a long night but, yeah . . . we . . ." Noah was having a hard time verbalizing the immensity of the conversation.

"We what?" Barney encouraged.

"We understand each other much better now," Noah understated.

"You're not going to steal my Chief of Staff from me, are you?" Barney said jokingly, trying to work the conversation around to getting a solid answer from Noah about accepting the position on *Epoch Utopia*.

Noah was too tired and emotionally drained to spar with him as was their normal way, so he plopped down on the couch and surrendered. "We talked it over and yes, you are losing us both."

Dr. Abus sat gently in the chair adjacent and tried to make sense of his mixed feelings, "You mean, you're going to accept the position?"

"Yes."

"And she accepted your proposal?"

"Yes."

"Congratulations, my good man!" Barney said with excitement, genuinely happy for the young couple. His excitement served to mask his concern and guilt about putting them in harm's way. For now, anyway.

"I can see you're tired," Barney said, finding a reason to excuse himself before his mixed emotions got the better of him. Lisa, even as cold and emotionless as she tried to be, had become like a daughter to him and now that he had caught a glimpse of the real Ruth, he foresaw a very difficult goodbye ahead.

"There should be a couple of suits to choose from in the closet," Abus said on his way out. "You'll need one for the press conference."

"What press conference?" Noah objected. The mere thought of standing in front all those people sent chills down his spine.

"Well, since you've accepted the position, I have to summon you to the announcement ceremony," Abus said, matter-of-factly. "By direct order of Supreme Leader Sargon. Don't worry. You can get about four hours of sleep, then get dressed, and meet me at my office."

The door closed behind him in eerie finality. Noah didn't bother moving to the bed. He just fell asleep there on the couch with his nose buried in the spot that still hinted of Ruth's hair.

CHAPTER ELEVEN

The darkness in the room made the flash photography seem as bright as the sun in comparison. It was a small room on purpose. There were much larger press rooms at the Palace complex—auditoriums even—but this announcement was to be particularly guarded and manipulated. A small, dark room meant they only had to deal with the very elite of the press while still creating the illusion of a large crowd pressing in on the great leader as a sea of faces trailing off into the infinite darkness.

Noah stood off to the side with Dr. Abus, waiting uncomfortably for the upcoming and unwanted moment of recognition. The room was so full that they had even pressed in around the side of the podium, pushing in behind Noah, Abus, and the rest of the leader's entourage. Noah was, of course, one of many new appointees being introduced to the public at this press conference, but he felt every camera flash as a spotlight directly meant for him. He clenched and released his toes repeatedly inside the unwelcome shoes restricting his feet in an unconscious attempt to relieve his social anxiety. The bodies chaotically pressing in around him, along with the noise and the flashing caused a déjà vu episode that made him forget where he was. All of a sudden, he was inside the dream he had been tortured by for months. Instead of seeing it from far above, he was just a face in the slithering mass.

The second the Supreme Leader entered the room and stepped to the podium, the press became a thundering, billowing throng of questions and gesturing attempts to get him to look toward each one's individual camera. This caused great turmoil within Noah, not just because of his social anxiety but because he instantly became aware of a dark presence in the room to which the others were oblivious.

Noah cringed as the reporter behind him yelled repeatedly in his ear, "Your Majesty . . . over here . . . TURN . . . this way . . ."

After several failed attempts to get Sargon to turn, the man shouted all the more excitedly as the Leader randomly turned their direction as a matter of course. As his line of sight scanned just over Noah's head, the reporter flashed his camera as he continued his mantra . . .

"TURN . . ."

This instant in time suddenly became infinite behind the dark eye of Sargon. As the flash created a halo around Noah's head, Sargon was thrust back into the imprisonment of his reoccurring nightmare. He was suddenly cringing back as *the face in the sun* was thundering for him to *TURN*.

Noah didn't understand what was happening. Sargon seemed to be looking right through him with an expression of horror which changed to one of fury as the gigantic figure charged toward him. In the small room, it was only a few strides for such a large man and this left Noah with only reflexes to rely on. As Sargon reached out, Noah ducked and rolled out of the way toward the podium which had been the only clear space in the crowded room but was now quickly filling with security officers.

Noah looked up from his humiliating position on the floor to see the reporter who had been screaming in his ear now dangling from the end of Sargon's arm like a limp flag. There was now much more chaos then before and the reporters were being shoved through the doors like cattle in a slaughterhouse.

The security detail of any other leader would have practically tackled and forcibly removed their protectee from a situation like this, but the Palace Security corps always took a different tack. They used sheer numbers to create an impenetrable circle of protection around him. They never, ever, touched him or directed him where to go. They merely created safe spaces for him to go to of his own accord.

Sargon came to his senses and realized the scene he was creating which made him even more furious. In one last burst of fury, he threw the man against the wall and stormed out the way he had come in.

Noah struggled to get up, but a security officer forced his face to the floor and held him there with a knee to the back of the head. He could see them handcuffing the man who had been thrown against the wall as he heard Barney's voice commanding Noah's release.

"He's with me! Let him go. He's not involved."

Involved with what? No one knew at this point, but whatever it was, it was sure to be news. It seemed as if they were going to cuff Noah as well and take him away until Dr. Abus's security chief got involved. The chief yanked Noah to his feet and with the help of the rest of his detail, whisked the two doctors out of the room the way Sargon had gone, practically carrying them.

When they reached a secure area, the two men tried to catch their breath and regain their bearings. Noah looked Barney directly in the eye with an expression that asked the question without words. Barney tried to act as if he were just as surprised as Noah about the whole situation, but Noah could sense, as he had often since their reunion, that Barney knew much more than he was letting on.

All of the cabinet ministers knew of Sargon's eccentricities. It was the reason they were always sure to walk on eggshells while in his presence. His public persona was well guarded with a picture painted by propaganda portraying him as virtuous, stable, and kind, but those in the inner circle knew that he was given to fits of rage and violence without warning. This episode would be covered over somehow or, since it took place in the presence of all of the world's media elites, painted from the opposite perspective.

Noah wisely bit his tongue while in the presence of Palace Security but fully intended to give Barney the *what for*, once they were alone again. He did not like being kept in the dark. So much so that it made him angry. But in Noah's normal, calculated way, he shelved the anger and started forming in his mind the questions to which he needed answers, as well as the apologetic he would have to present to Dr. Abus as to why he needed these answers, which was based around the fact that he cannot be expected to take on the responsibility of the safety of the colonists without access to all the data. He knew that in such a top-secret, information-guarded environment as the Palace, he would just be butting his head against a brick wall, but he formulated his argument all the same.

They were finally cleared to leave the secure area, so they made their way back to Dr. Abus's office with their security detail still on high alert. Sargon had such a tight grip on information flow that, although it had been an eternity—in news cycle time—since the incident, Ruth and the others back at the office had not seen or heard anything about it yet, except for the fact that their office security team said they were on lockdown and could not leave. As Noah felt, Ruth also hated not having all the information, especially in a situation like this where all one is told is that there is something dangerously wrong.

When Noah and Abus came through the door into the main office area, Ruth had to stop herself from running to them. It helped that Noah answered the concerned look on her face in his nonverbal way with an expression of calming assuredness.

"Is everything okay?" Ruth asked, as she quickly moved to eliminate the seeming chasm between them.

There was an awkward non-embrace between the newly engaged couple that stood out against the business-as-usual demeanor of Dr. Abus. Instead of answering her question, Noah gave her a covert look that let her know that he has much to tell her once they are alone. Dr. Abus simply continued on to his personal office with a nonchalant affirmation that everything is fine. Noah intended to follow him in and give him the *what for* he had been preparing, but he felt the need to stop and linger with Ruth, both to reassure her and to see what she knew about the surreal episode in which he had been caught up.

Just then, the breaking news graphic came up on the wall of the main office area. Ruth gave the command to unmute and they all watched and listened with interest.

"Moments ago, a mentally unstable terrorist, posing as a journalist, made an assassination attempt on the Supreme Leader at a press briefing . . ." was heard through the office sound system as dark images of the chaos flashed across the viewer.

". . . The dangerous assassin was subdued by none other than the Supreme Leader himself and is now in custody. Our great Leader showed unequaled bravery and resolve in the face of . . ." the report continued while Noah looked on in disgust.

"That's not what happened," Noah whispered in Ruth's ear with a little too much energy.

She shot a warning glare up to him, but he couldn't help the next sentence from slipping from his mouth.

"I was right there. There was no weapon . . . just a poor journalist in the wrong place at the wrong time."

Ruth locked her steely gaze to his and shook her head covertly to shut him up.

"Not here," she said with a tenth the energy he had whispered.

They both looked around nervously as if trying to find someplace to be alone when Noah noticed Ruth's face go white. He quickly gazed in the direction she had been looking when her countenance had changed then looked away just as quickly.

While the whole office had been distracted by the news feed, a man in a black suit had slipped in the back entrance and was sitting across the desk from Dr. Abus in his private office. Noah didn't exactly know what it meant, but he could tell from Ruth's reaction that such a visit was not good. Before they could attempt further to find a safe place to talk, Ruth received an incoming priority message. She slipped back into the persona of Lisa, the Chief of Staff, and excused herself to her personal office.

"Chief Keller, what can I do for you?" she asked in a tone of normalcy that gave Noah some insight into the person she had become during her time in the capital.

Noah could hear her conversation as she was walking away. He continued to watch the viewer and moved to the wall outside her office as if he were just looking for something to lean against while he watched when, in fact, he was just trying to get close enough to continue to hear.

"Yes, the profile is coming through now. Is this the right one? Yafeu Agymah Amadi?" Ruth asked, matter-of-factly.

She continued to listen intently as the chief described his dilemma. She immediately switched into problem-solving mode as she listened, running every scenario instantly in her mind. After a while she responded as reassuringly as she could.

"Well, Chief, with the priority code showing on this profile, I think we both know we're going to have to find some kind of solution. I have some ideas. Give me a couple of days to put together some options."

The chief thanked her with relief as they ended the communication. Relief was not at all what Ruth felt, as the responsibility to do the impossible once again fell to her, but she was confident she could solve this problem. It was impossible to feel relief while a certain man in black was sitting only meters away.

This is what she was thinking when she looked up to see that very man slither past her office and out the back entrance. She heard Abus call Noah into his office. Quickly but with dignity, she shot up and made her way to Abus's office where she took up post in the same manner Noah had outside hers. Her heart sank when she overheard Dr. Abus's serious voice.

"So, my friend, we have been summoned to the Palace."

CHAPTER TWELVE

Ruth felt reborn as Noah ushered her through the portal of the aircraft onto the tarmac of the travel port and into the familiar surroundings of the only place she ever really felt was home. Until now, she too had marooned herself on a solitary island. The emotional island of the guarded political operation of the capital. She had been holding back any and every glimpse of emotion behind a stone cold stoic dam for years now and she was filled to the brim. As soon as she saw Amala, Rajen, and the children waiting for them at the security gate, the dam broke. Amala ran to her and the two embraced, letting flow years of tears accompanied by a fury of high-pitched sentences unintelligible by the men even with translation software. The children hovered around them, vying for attention until they were acknowledged and eventually shooed into the back compartment of the Golkul family vehicle.

As they rode to Peter and Martha's, Ruth and Amala splashed from one subject to another at the speed of synapse, creating an N-dimensional web of thought that even the geniuses in the vehicle could not follow, nor could they get a word in edgewise. Noah and Rajen gave up on the endeavor and turned to the calmer seas of a private discussion of Rajen's results in confirming Noah's discoveries while on the island, until they were plunged back into the chaos with a gleeful squeal and a slap on Noah's shoulder.

"Why didn't you tell me, Noah?" Ruth almost yelled.

Noah and Rajen spun their seats around to face the women as the vehicle was in drone mode and needed no driver.

"Tell you what?" Noah said, having been oblivious to the conversation that had been going on behind him.

"That they submitted an application for crew status!" Ruth blurted with a *haven't you been listening* attitude.

"Well . . . first of all, I've been a little preoccupied!" Noah said with a similar *shouldn't you already be aware of this* attitude. "And second . . . isn't the real question *why haven't you told me?*"

"What do you mean?" Rajen interjected with some confusion.

"Well, I suppose you should be made aware of where I found *Ms. Evans* hiding. Right under my nose, actually," Noah said, still with a hint of disbelief lingering.

"What do you mean?" Rajen repeated, to the laughter of the women, since they had already had this conversation after the men had tuned them out.

"She is Chief of Staff to Dr. Abus. You know, the Palace Appointee in charge of human resources for the entire project!" Noah said sarcastically as he threw a glare Ruth's direction.

"That *is* strange . . ." Ruth pondered, returning to her professional self. "Their application never came across my desk."

She activated the viewer in her glasses and immediately started to search the files on the server back at her office. There was a brief delay as the security measures made sure of her identification since she was not on location. Instead of showing her impatience, she used the time to fill the others in on what she was doing.

"I'm trying to search for it now . . . okay, I'm in now . . . let me see . . ."

There was a long pause as the others waited silently.

"Well, there's a reason it never came across my desk," Ruth said with some frustration. "It's not here."

"What do you mean?" Rajen said, trying to sound more surprised than angry or disgusted.

"Don't worry," Ruth said in a tone that elicited faith. "We'll get to the bottom of it."

"I don't want to speak out of turn . . ." Noah said, half joking, ". . . but we do have a direct line to the one who has the final say on these things."

Noah sent a quick prayer up while allowing the others to believe he was referring to Dr. Abus.

"I'll have to filter down through the servers of the sub-committees that feed our department. It may take some time, but I'll find you," Ruth reassured them.

"How many committees does it have to go through?" Noah asked with clear contempt for bureaucracy.

"Well, depending on who they first filed with . . . it could have gone through any number of departments, but . . . they all have to go through the PCAR at some point so . . . let me start there."

As soon as Noah heard Ruth mention the Palace Council on Academic Resources, he had a suspicious gnawing feeling in the pit of his stomach. He glanced at Rajen and could tell that he too was holding back suspicion. They both knew who had recently been appointed to the PCAR and they both knew Kent Stewart all too well.

Amala could see that her husband was starting to turn stoic and noticed the covert looks of understanding between the two men.

"What are you not telling me, Rajen?" Amala scolded.

"It's nothing," he answered dismissingly.

"*It's nothing* is different than *nothing* . . ." she said accusingly. "*Nothing* means nothing. *It's nothing* means . . . well, there is something, but you're calling *something*, nothing. What is it, Rajen?"

"Dr. Stewart has been appointed to the PCAR," Noah answered for him as he could see his friend trailing down dark thoughts behind his eyes.

"Well, that's good then, right?" Amala perked with too much optimism for the situation.

"Yeah, it's fine . . ." Rajen managed to say without anything resembling optimism.

"*Fine* is not *good*, Rajen," his wife retorted. "What's wrong?"

"It is fine, really . . ." Noah inserted, trying to appease her. "Dr. Stewart is just a little, well . . ." Noah looked to Rajen for some help choosing an apt adjective.

"A little what?" Amala asked, losing some optimism.

Seeing that Rajen was not going to help, Noah finally confessed, "A little petty and possibly jealous."

"What does he have to be jealous about?" Amala argued as if she could change the reality of the situation with her words. "He's too old to be chosen for the crew anyway."

"It's not really about that . . ." Noah trailed off as he looked to Ruth for a solution, knowing she always had many for every situation.

Ruth picked up on the meaning of Noah's nonverbalization, as she had learned to do and reassured the increasingly hopeless couple with an ironic, "Don't worry about it." As *worrying* was the reason why she always had several solutions waiting.

"Dr. Abus can clear this up," Noah half asked, half assumed, trying to help Ruth reassure them.

"You all just let me worry about it," Ruth said trying to sound like they were all making a big deal over nothing while knowing that Dr. Abus could not be seen as showing favoritism and that if Stewart was really able to make an argument for their rejection to the rest of the members of the PCAR, for whatever personal reasons, it would take an immense amount of political capital to overcome. The fact that Noah and Dr. Abus had been summoned to the Palace in the manner they were added to her doubts about the strength of his political capital at the moment. The summons could be about any number of things, but anyone *in the know* in the Cabinet staff knew at least this one thing—a visit from one of *the Three* was not a good thing. The meeting with Sargon was imminent as far as the Palace calendar went. Impending was a more apt description as far as Ruth was concerned. Comparing Palace time to emotional time was much like comparing geologic time to a stopwatch. The Supreme Leader had a full schedule all the time. A summons to the Palace came with a specific time—days, sometimes weeks in advance. Not that the Leader couldn't alter his schedule on a whim, he often did, but he liked for his subjects to have plenty of time to stew in their own nervous worrying about what the great Sargon would want of them. He increased his surveillance of the subject during this time because they often acted out of guilt and revealed information he could make use of during the audience. Noah had one week to prepare for this impending convergence. *Epoch Utopia* was to depart shortly after, so they had not one, but two impossible-to-anticipate collisions with destiny to prepare for. With those things looming, they had no choice but to wrap up their earthly lives with diligence and haste in the short time remaining. As she was learning to do, Ruth put aside worries about the upcoming meeting with the Supreme Ruler and refocused on trying to solve Rajen and Amala's problem.

The mood in the vehicle seemed overly somber now, as compared to the jubilee of reunion the trip had started out as. It wasn't long before they reached their destination and the jubilee began again.

Despite Peter's every effort to keep Martha in her chair as they waited expectantly. She of course refused and, with almost a sixth sense, her slow journey to the front of the house ended just in time for her to see them pull in the drive. Ruth hurried to Martha as she stood in the open door and they embraced as tears flowed freely. Peter could not wait for his own turn.

He wrapped his strong arms meekly around the two women and hid his own tears in the tops of their heads.

Noah felt complete as he witnessed a true picture of love and grace, for truly, both Ruth and he had caused the pain of the prodigal to be visited upon these gentle souls and yet, there was not an ounce of condemnation present in this reunion. Perhaps the news of a wedding would cover over the pain of telling them that they were once again leaving. This time forever.

* * *

The wedding was small but beautiful. Peter was Ruth's great-uncle, but, as it was for Noah, he was the closest thing to a father that she had since she lost her parents. Since Peter was performing the service, Dr. Abus was happy to walk Ruth down the aisle in his place. It was a particularly moving moment for Abus. Not only was he sending another one of those he cared for into the unknown dangers of space, never to return, but he was also losing his right hand. Surrogate father or no, it was not as if he could grab hold of the old adage that he's not losing a daughter, he's gaining a son. He was losing them both. He tried not to think about the constant reminder of their absence that he was bound to have. Abus could barely function without Ruth, and anyone trying to fill her shoes was sure to be nothing but a reminder of her absence. He was so impressed with her that, now that she was going to be on *Epoch Utopia*, there was no question that he would appoint her to the equivalent of his position on the vessel. It had never entered her mind to apply for crew status, but when Noah came back into the picture, she knew that her place was at his side. At his side yes, but in a sense, she would be his boss. Abus was going to tell them as a wedding gift. He smiled as he thought about the last laugh he was going to have on Noah with that news.

Ruth beamed with joyful beauty as she grasped Dr. Abus's arm and slowly marched down the aisle. She lost her breath at her first glimpse of Noah as he stood with patient longing. He had surprised her by shaving his beard and cutting off his pony tail. His resolute jaw line had been hidden for so many years, but the smile it held was not unfamiliar, just amplified. His short, kempt hair now framed an expression of joy on his face, where his former style would have done its best to conceal any emotion. Years of concealing emotion herself now took their toll as she started bawling before they even made it halfway down the aisle. Abus patted her hand softly as it rested on his forearm and slipped her the decorative silk kerchief from his jacket pocket as they made it to the front. As the veil raised, Noah took his own and meekly patted beneath her eyes, somehow knowing not to smudge her makeup. His gentle, caring gesture was like the whisper of *I've got you* in the ear of someone falling into strong and trusted arms.

The ceremony was a blur to them both, but they did manage to glean from Peter's wisdom as he briefly addressed them in love in front of the small gathering.

". . . for this reason a man shall leave his father and mother and be joined to his wife, and the two shall become one flesh . . ." Peter paused and looked deeply into the eyes of each, with eyes that seemed to smile all by themselves, before he continued with some wise personal commentary, ". . . this is a deep truth that far too many have glossed over at a time like this. A time when we're all happy and bursting with the emotions that come along with love but are not love . . . a time when the rest of life is framed with ideals and placed on a pedestal for all to see. I am so blessed to be able to share this time with you . . ." Peter's eyes welled up slightly while Martha could be heard sobbing audibly in the front row, overcome with thankfulness that she was able to fight off her disease long enough to be present for this day. ". . . but this time is only the beginning of a long journey together. Please don't miss this foundational truth at this time of carefree celebration. You are no longer two but one. This is now your reality . . . your context . . . your gift . . . your privilege. To enter into marriage with a grasp of the wonderful power of this is to enter armed against failure and the horrific pain that comes from ripping one flesh back into two pieces. At a time like this, we celebrate the joy and pleasure of two individuals uniting into one new flesh but often overlook the reality of this very thing. There will be times when one, the other, or both of you will not feel like loving. This is inevitable. When you unite one imperfect man to one imperfect woman, you get imperfection times two by very definition, but you also get joy times two and pleasure times two and laughter times two . . . love times two. When that time comes, you must remember that you are no longer two but one. Don't lie to yourself about this reality, that only causes pain. Decide to love . . . decide to love and I guarantee that, on the other side of that decision, you will experience love and life in a new dimension . . . one you never could have imagined before the love of pure will. Even the fuzzy feelings you're experiencing today will reappear if you decide to love with the love of pure will." He paused briefly and looked out into the crowd. "With that . . . Therefore, what God has joined together, let no man separate."

Peter's words were sobering yet he was so authentically joyful that everyone present hung on his every word. It was as if he were a master painter of words who was skilled in using the technique of shading. With the darker words, he brought depth and focus to the subject of the masterpiece, pulling light and beauty out of negative space. Many present saw the ancient beauty of marriage for the first time. To think of love as an act of the will was a thought process almost extinct in a culture of egocentric hedonism. The feelings that were mistaken for love were most often succumbed to because they simply could not be resisted. Those feelings eventually faded, leaving the so-called lovers to move on to greener pastures in search of their ever-evasive happiness. To experience the love of someone deciding to love them was a very rare thing in a culture where even the traditional roll of the family had been usurped by a cold, heartless government bureaucracy. Although people seemed to expand their social network further than any other time in history, through social media technologies of every sort, they were not really connected to anyone on any sort of tribal level. That kind of interdependence was frowned upon by the powers that be. Any dependence was skillfully rerouted toward Sargon's bureaucracies, leaving the bonds of family and true friendship weak enough to be broken and replaced with the chains of his agenda.

Love, family, and friendship had not completely died out yet, but it was certainly on the ropes. This small gathering was witnessing what was in a sense, a reintroduction of an endangered species into their society. Only time would tell if such a tame creature as true love could compete and survive in such a savage emotional wilderness.

For Noah and Ruth, time was now on their side. They were already best friends, so there was no having to get to know the real person behind the usual dating mask. It was the fact they had gotten to know each other so well that scared Noah off in the first place. Until now, time seemed to be running against him as he had been searching desperately for Ruth, but this ceremony served as a declaration to all present that they would put time in its place and grow old together. That they were about to leave everything and everyone they have ever known behind to float off into space together only served to strengthen their bond and increase love's chances of overcoming societal norms of semi-permanent relationships and self-gratifying wandering. The journey they were about to embark on was in no way semi-permanent, but somehow the weight of that looming over them was lessened by their decision to declare their love as also, in no way semi-permanent.

And so the journey began.

EPILOGUE

The darkness, welcome as it was, could not cover the exposed insanity of the emperor of the known universe. Sleep eluded Sargon once again as he lay staring at the ceiling of his bed chamber. Every time he closed his eyes, he could see nothing but the shining face in the sun. After one last attempt at closing his eyes, he growled angrily at the women sleeping on his bed to get out. They woke abruptly and raced out in reasonable fear.

Once he was alone, the giant arose and searched in the dark for the hidden release that opened the secret door leading to his personal surveillance chamber. The technicians who had installed it were now dead and although it tapped into the technology created by the Three, even they did not know of its existence.

If he could not find solace in sleep, he would mask the very need for solace with the trappings of power. He sat in the dark with only the dim glow of the halo-emitters revealing the truth of who he had become—a man possessed by obsession itself. He searched for hours for any detail on Dr. Noah McAdams, for any clue as to why the torturous imagery of his nightmare converged upon this one man. Every search ended in frustration. This one did not conform to his grand scheme. Dr. McAdams did not become addicted to the convenience of Sargon's technology nor was he deceived by its misleading path toward Sargon's agenda as the rest of the world had been.

Having gathered whatever information he could, the obsessed madman morphed back into the Great Leader of his public persona. As he stood to begin his day, his majestic form and dignified expression served to mask the one thought at the forefront of his mind, *McAdams would have to be dealt with the old-fashioned way.*

ACKNOWLEDGMENTS

This book would not have been possible without the encouragement and support of so many family and friends that it is impossible to name them all here. You know who you are. Melissa, you put up with the seasons in which seemingly all of my spare time was consumed by the creative and editing process of this book. It is my wish that you also share in the rewarding experience of the finished product. Mom, you showed the excitement and encouragement that only a mother could. Hopefully, this book is not a work only an author's mother could love. Dad, you taught me to keep on keeping on. This book would not have been possible without that lesson. Cris, Kevin, Linda, and Kay, all my life I have been inspired by your artistic endeavors and your loving encouragement. Greg and Phoebe, it was your first look at this project that set me on a serious path toward its conclusion. You convinced me that I had something worth sharing with the world and that I had the ability to share it with unique quality. Lastly, thanks to my editor, Amanda Sauer—you took this dyslexic introvert and guided him through the wilderness that is mass communication through the English language in written form. I truly could not have done it without your expertise and insight into good storytelling. Thank you all.

JEFFERYDALECOLE.COM

To see more from author Jeffery Dale Cole, visit jefferydale-cole.com. In addition to updates on the release of the next book in The Babel Resurgence series, you can enjoy music, photography, and short articles.

BUILDING SPACE

Building Space is a training program that helps clarify the thought process necessary for understanding your purpose. It provides practical steps to building space in your life for the important things as well as personal mentorship and encouragement. To apply, visit jefferydalecole.com/BuildingSpace.

THE BUILDING SPACE

The Building Space is Jeffery's regular live webcast that explores the ancient principles necessary to building space in your life for the important things. To join the private group, visit jefferydalecole.com/Live.

DALINE.BIZ

If you have a desire to live a healthier, more abundant life, then you may benefit from one or more of the opportunities found at Daline.biz. Tell us about yourself at Daline.biz/Contact. We can help.